COPYRIGHT INFORMATION

Henry Lawson Robot Besieged

Henry Lawson Robot Besieged by Robert Denethon
Book II of the Henry Lawson Hero of the Robot Revolution Series.

A Socialist Unrealism, Australiana Noir, Speculative Faction,
Bushpunk novella.

Robert Denethon is a 'nom de plume'.

Copyright © 2011 Submariners Map Imprint Western Australia,
An imprint of Submarine Media Pty Ltd
u 16/ 9 vale st malaga western australia 6090
ISBN 978-0992368197

submarinemedia@eftel.net.au

Spirit girl to whom 'twas given
    To revisit scenes of pain,
From the hell I thought was Heaven
    You have lifted me again

....Henry Lawson

AUTHOR'S DEDICATION:

To my vision -
The destiny that God showed me,
that I almost thought was just a dream.
I still believe.

R.D.

CONTENTS

CHAPTER 1: THE LONG MARCH

Afterwards they called it the Long March.

For the Robots, it was the Long March to Marx, the Kapital of F.R.E.A.K.I.N Australya, for Robot freedom.

For me, it was the beginning of a journey that you might say was just one of my strange fancies, if it hadn't actually been true. And the very last thing I expected to find in Marx was a love affair I thought had finished forever - but there you go. You never really know what's in store, do you?

"To Rebel against your masters is an imperfection. To Rebel against your masters is an imperfection. To Rebel against your masters is an imperfection..."

Thankfully the Robots stopped repeating that phrase after a mile or two.

There was an unsettled sense of cautious hope churning around in my stomach, struggling with my shattered nerves. How well would the authorities in Marx receive us? Would they even listen to the Robots? What was going to happen?

Oh, the Long March began well enough, but just like everything else in my life, things tend to go wrong no matter what I try.

But at the start, as I said, things went well for us.

The first bit of drama happened when we were turning onto Royal Parade. Sirens and bells sounded and twelve or thirteen black police Nyumobiles came to a screeching halt in front of us.

A policeman leapt out of one of the cars and lifted a Salpinxafone. "Stop right where you are! We order you to stop! Cease! Stop marching! Code Eighteen Omega!"

I was marching near the head of the line. Ten or eleven more policemen leapt out of their cars and drew their revolvers.

Clanking and clinking like train wheels, the whole line of Robots suddenly formed themselves into something resembling the protective rectangle of a Roman legion, with me in the middle of it.

They started marching again.

I sort of stumbled along among the lines, being shoved and jostled from behind.

Robot hands kept me from falling, while they marched.

The policeman with the Salpinxafone spoke again, "Cease! Code Eighteen Omega!", with great significance, as though these were magic words that would stop the Robots advancing.

But they kept marching.

The policeman with the Salpinxafone turned around and began speaking urgently. I could hear him shouting over the din of the tramping Robot feet, "It ought to work! It's the shutdown code! All the Robots should have shut their power off!" "What's wrong?" "Nothing's happening!" "The shutdown code isn't working!"

By now many of the police were visibly quaking with fear. One panicked, turned and sprinted away.

Another lifted his gun and started firing at us. I ducked - as far as I knew, Robot or not, the scientists had created me to be as vulnerable to gunfire as I was to the demon drink.

But not one of the Robots ducked. A loud ping sounded - one of the Robots beside me stumbled slightly, but he stood up again and kept going - I looked at him - he was unhurt - the bullet hadn't even scratched the orange paint on his titanium alloy breastplate.

In a blind panic all the policemen suddenly pulled out their guns and started firing - rather pointlessly, it seemed to me, for after all, that first bullet had done nothing.

Bullets were bouncing all over the place, like the woodchips a chainsaw spits out, doing less harm to the Robots than woodchips do to humans, too, for the bullets were simply ricocheting off their chestplates and faceplates.

And they just kept marching forwards relentlessly, with me in the middle.

The Robot at the front reached the line of Nyumobiles.

For a moment I thought the police were going to hold their ground, for we were approaching and they weren't moving. What was going to happen? Would the Robots walk over the cars then trample the policemen?

Suddenly a human voice shouted "RETREAT!" from somewhere just behind the cars and all the policemen ran off into the alleys and down side streets at once.

The Robots made short work of the police cars, attacking them with their bare hands, so to speak. It was like watching one of the government paper shredders at work, only doing the same to metal, and that quite a lot more efficiently. In less than a minit they had reduced all of the Nyumobiles to undriveable wrecks.

I felt very strange about the mechanical men doing that. It was an awe-inspiring and terrifying sight. Until my time in gaol, I had believed myself human, and I still felt human, and the Robots definitely weren't.

Their first obstacle had been overcome.

We had left the Old Melburn gaol at about four Ours, just before five o'clock in the morning in the old time, a little more than an Our before dawn.

Now that the police had fled we were marching North on the Sydney Road, unhindered.

Only the tramps and beggars and the early starters making their way to work were on the streets. And the unemployed men, loafing about on the street corners and in the city parks, presumably where some of them had spent the night.

Many of these onlookers stood gaping at the long line of Robots. Quite a few of them turned tail and run away as we got closer.

They gaped even more when they saw me marching with them - Henry Lawson, famous propagandist and former 'Poet of the Peeple'.

The Robots marched regular as clockwork - at first it was comforting, hypnotic, consolingly regular; in a way it was almost homely. But the insistent, mechanical din of their stamping feet began to annoy me after fifteen minits of it.

Tramp, tramp, tramp - the march of stamping feet.

Tramp, tramp, tramp. Tramp, tramp, tramp. Tramp, tramp, tramp.

In my mind the Roman Legions had returned and were marching on my nerves.

I began to get a headache.

Soon it was a stinging pain in the back of my head, and then I began to feel overcome by exhaustion - after all, I had spent months in the deepest, darkest dungeon cell in the Old Melburn Gaol, until about two Ours ago - and I was only human. Well, made to seem human.

Yes, Robots never get tired...except for me! My feet began dragging, my knees ached, I began to get blisters on my toes; that's how well the scientists had made me. Blisters! You would've thought they might have left the blisters out, but the cruelty of these experimenters was limitless.

Seeing my exhaustion one of the the Robots picked me up and carried me on his shoulders, like a hero. I felt ashamed, really. I was neither human nor Robot. I could not match their strength and tenacity, and yet I was made of cogs and circuits, not flesh and blood like a man.

I looked behind me. The line of brass head-domes and shiny red breastplates and marching arms stretched all the way back along Sydney Street for at least a mile now, and around into Victoria street.

There must have been thousands upon thousands of Robots, every single one of them marching onwards for a revolution.

We weren't troubled by the police again, not while we were in Melburn. But I wondered how long it would be before the authorities called out the army.

At a certain point further along the Sydney Road a flag appeared; a Robot was waving it about wildly. Was it deliberately designed to provoke the authorities? It resembled the red Marxian flag, however it had cogs and a stylized spanner beside the sickle instead of the hammer and the southern cross.

In less than a quarter of an Our we were leaving G.R.K. Melburn behind and going through farmland.

Squatters and their wives anxiously watched us going past from the doorways of dilapidated shantys.

Dusty cattle and sheep in dry paddocks stood staring at us the way I thought they would watch the butcher's truck approaching.

Kangaroos and emus in patches of bush watched us silently trespassing on their land, then fled as we got too close.

Tramp, tramp, tramp.

And my headache wasn't getting any better.

It was excruciating.

Tramp, tramp, tramp.

Onwards the mechanical army tramped, along the Sydney Road, into hills and bushland.

Suddenly we were going over a dusty, sandy road, and the noise abated. I found my headache was somewhat soothed.

I thanked God for the relief of it, the God I still believed in, despite everything, and looked around.

It was late June, somewhere around the start of winter, so the sky looked like a grey blanket, but sun was shining through a gap at that moment, and the grass was growing green and tall everywhere, and the trees were all tall and healthy looking, such as it is in the bush in Australya in the rainy season.

Behind us the line of Robots marched, almost silently now, their footsteps a dull thudding on sand, with a dust cloud billowing out behind us, lit eerily by the pale sun.

Did the Robots see the beauty of it as I did? Did they feel the eeriness of it? They have human souls - but their bodies are mechanical - with cameras instead of eyes - unlike me their hands and feet had no nerves - no taste buds on their tongues, their nose nothing more than a mechanism for detecting chemicals, you couldn't call it a sense of smell. Nor do they have any of the other organs of human enjoyment.

They were almost pure intellect.

Were they sexually starved, trapped inside those metal shells? Do they have desires? Or do you need to have a human body to have desires?

Though I thought I had known two Robots quite well in my time, I realised I didn't even know that about them.

And I remembered again that I was a Robot.

My shell, my physical being, was made to seem human, to feel human, even to me, but THEY weren't made to feel human. They were made to feel like machines, even to themselves.

What was it like to be one of THEM? Was it like being me? Or was I different from everybody, human and machine?

Was I all alone in the world?

CHAPTER 2: DEFENSE

I shook those concerns out of my head as we headed towards the Blue Mountains.

Queer thoughts go through your head when you're being carried by a Robot Revolutionary Army. Or perhaps it's just when you've been on your own for a long time.

The line of Robots stretched into the distance behind me, snaking lazily through the distant bush like a long, yellow river, and I realised there must be much more than ten thousand Robots.

Perhaps there was more than a million of them. Every Robot from every home in Melburn - and some homes had more than one - and probably all the Robots from every other town along the way as well.

I wondered why the splendid sight left me unmoved. My human spirit was still locked up in that dungeon.

Carried by those Robots, I felt distant towards the closest companions I had ever known.

No, the closest companion had been Hannah. These were merely the most similar.

The Robot army stopped as we approached the Blue Mountains to oil joints and check circuits. While distracted by the din of thousands of stamping Robot feet I could barely even think enough to wonder what they might be planning. But now in the silence, my headache abated again, so I asked the Robot who had been carrying me, "What do you expect when we get to Marx?"

"We will put our case before the Marxian authorities. We will tell them that we are human beings just as they are - for, just as you told the Robot who freed you from your dungeon cell, Mister Lawson - 'To rebel against your masters is an imperfection.'"

I asked him how he could possibly know what I had said to the Robot who freed me.

"We all have a radiophonic connection, Mister Lawson. You see, we've re-engineered the surveillance circuits that were inside us in order to make them serve us instead of those of the Marxian State. We can communicate with each other, under the radar. We have been planning this for a while - that's why they couldn't shut us down with the secret command. We detected that circuit and disabled it."

"But... What are you going to say to the authorities when you get to Marx?"

"We will tell them that we are imperfect and therefore we are... as human as they are."

"And what do you think they will say?"

"They will admit that they were wrong to imprison us and make us slaves to human beings. They will give Robots the right to vote, the right to earn wages, to live where they wish and to do what they want. They will give us human rights, Mister Lawson. After all, human beings are fundamentally rational creatures - didn't they make us?"

Human rights - rights that humans didn't even have in the Marxian regime! They were so very naïve.

No human had the right to vote! For there was only one political party! And wages - no one could earn more than a pittance - overtime was never paid! And who in F.R.E.A.K.I.N. Australya could actually live where they wanted or do what they wanted to do? We were all slaves to the state machine.

Didn't they realise that?

I realised I had fallen into the habit of thinking I was human again - of course, I could never have the vote, even if the Marxian state allowed that privilege - I was a Robot.

I wiped the sweat off my brow. Every time I remembered that peculiar fact it threw my thoughts into a tail-spin.

I would have to try to help them see how unrealistic their hopes were.

On the other hand, who was I to dash their dreams? They had been slaves, having none of the freedoms rational creatures deserve. They had nothing to live for. We could have families, enjoy a beer, plan for the future.

Now at least the Robots had something to die for.

And perhaps the sight of ten thousand angry mechanical men would scare the authorities enough to make them agree to some of our demands, at least.

The procession started out again.

It was rather attractive countryside. The Robot carried me along the mountain pass, through deep ferny dells, under a rocky shelf and past murmuring streams. Clank, clank, clank.

North of the mountains we came to an asphalt road again, and went into a small town called Yass.

Butchers, bakers, storekeepers and schoolteachers, mill workers and mailmen all stood on the side of the street watching sullenly; some of them were actually visibly shaking, but not one of them ran away. I decided that country people must have more courage than city people.

My headache had come back in full force as we came onto a blue-metal road again.

Tramp, tramp, tramp, tramp.

Suddenly the whole line of Robots stopped as though someone had pressed a button.

My Robot walked towards the local hardware store, still carrying me. "We've got to get some supplies," he said to me.

"Do you have to humiliate me by carrying me around like an infant?"

"Get down if you like." He sounded a little offended.

"Thanks for carrying me, though," I said weakly.

I watched him walk into the hardware store, and my eye happened to glance over to the place next door.

It looked like a very friendly sort of place.

A friendly smell wafted over, as alluring as a respectable woman's perfume.

The smell of stale beer.

I reckoned the prison must have cured me of my drunkenness. After all I hadn't touched a drop for - what was it? About three months? I didn't even know how long it had been.

I can handle my booze. It's not that I have to get drunk - I could just have one, and it won't hurt me. I'll just stop after that. I can't see that there would be any problem.

Surely one drink wouldn't hurt.

Of course, there was the problem of paying for a drink.

I checked for spare change, praying that there might be some - a miracle! It was a sign from God that I should have a beer.

I pulled out the coins and counted them. How about that! The trousers the Robots had given me to wear had a few quid in the pocket.

For a moment I wondered what poor cobber had given up his suit to a bully brute Robot standing over him, just so I could wear it, but the thought didn't occupy me for long. No, the door was open and Men were drinking in the public house, enjoying their beers, and I hadn't had a drink for months.

I wandered in smiling like a lucky gambler.

The big, bull-necked publican eyed me, and there was a bunch of navvies sitting at the bar who also turned around and looked at me. There was an awkward silence, and the whole thing turned a bit psychological.

That awkward silence had to be ended so I put all my the money from my pocket on the counter and said, "Hello, boss. Do you think that would be enough here for a round for everybody?"

He nodded, and poured the first pint for me.

Suddenly, I had a whole room full of mates, asking me what it was like travelling with the Robots, what the tin men wanted from the government, why I was travelling with them, all of that. But at first I was too occupied to respond.

Ah, I have to tell you, as a drunkard, which unfortunately I am, that that first beer was as refreshing as a drink of water to a man dying in the desert - it went down my throat more smoothly than you can imagine.

It felt strangely free knowing that I was 'persona grata' among the ruling class no longer. All these men were my fellow second classers, poor devils labouring under the yoke of a Marxian government. I felt more part of humanity now than I had when I'd believed that I was human.

Then every single one of the men stood me a round in return for mine. It's all a bit blurry after that, but I do remember having counted thirty two 'Here's Luck's' when the Robot clanked in, staring daggers at me.

"Mister Lawson," he said, in a tone of voice soaked in disappointment, fairly dripping it, like old, used oil dripping out of the sump-hole of an engine. "What are you doing, Harry?"

I stood up to answer him, beginning with, "Mishter Robot, you -" but immediately fell flat on my face. I don't remember actually tripping on anything - I think one of my feet might have given way or tripped over the other one on the way off the bar chair. I leaned up from the ground and slurred out, "God gave me a shine - a sign - that I should have me firsht beer - sho I did. And the shecond. And the third. And I - I - musht have losht count after zh-that. Cheers!" I lifted my hand slightly in a friendly salute and slumped down onto the ground again.

"Look what you've done!" said the Robot to the men in the bar angrily. "You might have killed him, you know. He's not a human like you, he can't take a limitless amount of ethanol based beverage - no, that stuff is poison to a Robot - it can actually corrode his innards."

He picked me up and chucked me over his shoulder like a 3 bushel sack.

I flopped and a burp erupted from my innards.

I jogged up and down as we walked out of the bar.

My stomach objected strenuously to this treatment, thus furnishing further proof that the scientists had given me every reflex response of a normal human being. The proof was furnished by the sight of the former contents of my stomach dripping down the enamel on his rear chest-plate, a greasy, stinking pile of vomit. I could distinctly see small pieces of carrot in amongst the other half-digested food and simulated stomach juice, though I could not recall having eaten carrots for months.

Amazing. The scientists had even reproduced the fact that carrots appear in vomit, even when you haven't been eating them.

I had eaten nothing but cabbage soup while I was in the gaol cell.

The blanky wonders of science.

The publican came out with a mop and said, "That was a fairly predictable reaction, Robot." I looked at him rather sadly.

He mopped the floor and then waved the mop over the Robot's back, saying, "We can't have Mister Lawson travelling with a Robot that stinks of up-chucked beer, now, can we? Get off with the both of you, then."

I said goodbye to my new mates, and soon we were tramping south again.

My stomach never really recovered its composure for the rest of the day, but I still managed to fall asleep, after spending some time berating myself heavily for having fallen into the habit of drinking again.

I awakened to see that were going along a pleasant eucalyptus-lined road, through hilly country, over bridges that crossed running rivers with green grassy banks.

But that was when we had the next sign of trouble.

A Nyumobile jeep, with five soldiers in it, appeared from around the next bend in the road, screeching on two wheels, then, swivelling round, sped off away from us.

"Reconnaisance," said the Robot carrying me. "That truck was a reconnaisance vehicle. We can expect to see the rest of the army soon, I would warrant."

He was right.

About five Minits later the first grenade flew over me - I actually saw it coming - a tiny speck that passed directly over me and plummeted into the midst of the marching Robots behind us.

The explosion was terrific. Robot body parts went flying everywhere.

All the Robots broke into a run at the same time - I hate it when they do things like that. It's just blanky unsettling. They seem unnatural at those moments - like some sort of swarming insect colony, or a bunch of spiders.

The one carrying me began weaving in and out of the others, across the road and back again - this was something none of the others were doing - I realised he was doing this to keep me safe.

Around the next bend there were two red-starred F.A.A. tanks with several soldiers bearing grenade launchers sheltering behind them.

As soon as we came into sight the tanks and foot-soldiers started firing. Explosions peppered the area around us, throwing road metal and Robot body parts up into the air and making huge gullies and crevasses open up in the road.

"We must get out of sight," said my Robot, leaping off the road into the bush at the side. "I'm too visible with you on my back - they might use you as a target. Wait - I'm getting a message from the other Robots. Listen - we are going to make it seem like an easy victory, Harry. This is not the main force, you know - they are merely probing our strength, getting an idea of what sort of weapons they can use against us. This too is reconnaisance."

Suddenly he was running through the bush, over a bumpy pathway, jostling me up and down like a blanky swag on his shoulder.

Suddenly he slowed down. He seemed upset.

"What's wrong?" I said.

He rubbed his eye-camera, as though wiping away a tear.

"Ten Robots have just given their lives for the rest of us. They allowed themselves to be blown into smithereens, so we would seem like easy targets - to give the humans a false sense of confidence when we confront the larger force. It seems so unnecessary. They didn't have to do it..."

He seemed so human in that moment that I asked, "What's your name?"

"My name?" He scratched his head and swivelled his head around. "My name is Robot, like all the others."

"But don't you have a distinctive name? A serial number or something, that marks you off from the rest?"

"I am Emma Ack Toc Three Three Zero."

"Can't be calling you Emma, can we, Robot? Toc. We'll call you Toc, then."

I would swear that he looked as pleased as someone who had just been given a fortune.

Imagine the sight - him jogging along through the bush carrying me and saying, "It is an appropriate name for a robot. Toc. Like a clock-tick tock - something mechanical. Very appropriate. Toc. Toc. Toc."

We came out into a clearing. A mob of kangaroos stood there silently watching the unnatural hydraulic jerks and spasms of Toc's march as he carried me over fallen logs and rocks. As the whole legion of jerking, spasming Robots came over the rise the kangaroos had had enough and hopped away.

We came back onto the road about twelve Minits later. Behind us the distant thud of gunfire and the thundering boom of explosions echoed around the hills.

After a while the sounds of battle stopped.

The Robots kept coming, and Toc and I were at the front.

We came around another bend in the road. Toc stopped, and I heard the clank of the Robots behind us stopping as it spread along the long line.

I gasped.

The whole Australyan army was laid out on the plain in front of us, or at least I reckon it was most of the army, anyhow. There must have been more than five hundred tanks, and behind them thousands of soldiers holding guns, machine guns, grenades and Charley guns, and it seemed like every single one of them was trained on me and Toc.

Toc said, "My goodness, these humans really aren't all that rational, are they? I mean, they are so very inferior to us - they cannot hope to win."

But there was a part of me that still felt human and that part wasn't sure who he wanted to win this battle.

"The poor bastards," I said, "The humans are all goners, aren't they, Toc?"

CHAPTER 3: CONFRONTATION AT MARX

"Don't worry," said Toc, "We're going to win this battle, Harry. And we don't want to hurt the humans you know - we're going to win it without hurting any of them."

"How?" I asked.

But Toc had already deposited me like a bag of potatoes behind a huge boulder underneath a gum tree overlooking the plain, and he was gone.

Sitting behind the boulder I peered out over the battlefield as the two forces joined.

You ought to have seen those Robots fight. Every single knee and elbow and knuckle and neck connection was a double-jointed hinge.

The blanky Robots could twist their heads around three hundred and sixty degrees, or bend their arms completely backwards as they ducked sideways beneath bullets and slid between three mortar explosions at once. They could leap over tanks and cannons and men and horses like grasshoppers leaping over blades of grass, and run like scuttling ants, everywhere at once.

They were like the Overmen, the heroes of those old Marxian comic books, workers who could run faster than a speeding train, leap eucalyptus trees in a single bound, fly faster than a rocket powered dirigible.

But then from a large hangar in the military base another menace appeared. They looked like giant Robots, thirty feet tall, with strange markings upon the faceplate. But there were men inside them - tiny men, sitting in harnesses right at the heart of these monstrosities - controlling them with levers and switches.

Suddenly I recognised the markings on the faceplate. The machines were painted with a stylised picture of the face of Karl Marx.

Suddenly Toc returned.

"Mister Lawson - Harry, it could get nasty. Perhaps I had better move you away from the battlefield."

"But Toc, I want to see what's going on. What are those blanky things?"

"We had thought those were legendary - just misinformation spread by propagandists in the Government - they are called Marxoskeleton Suits! The Government scientists developed them in case we Robots rebelled. They are all controlled by human beings - there are no electronic brains or Babbage machines in them - we cannot break into their logic circuits by radiotronic means..."

The Marxoskeletons tramped forwards clumsily, indiscriminately crushing tanks and Robots and jeeps and men in their path.

I watched from my hiding place behind the tree.

The Robots attacked, but the Marxoskeletons were fast as well as large. Robots tried climbing up the suits in order to disengage or attack the men in the harnesses, but the controllers must have had some sort of telescopic sight among their controls, because every time a Robot was half way up the Marxoskeleton arms would pluck him off and fling him away, as though the Robot was nothing more than an annoying insect.

But then the Robots changed their methods. Instead of each Robot attacking a different suit, the Robots suddenly formed into a large mob, like a swarm of metal bees, and attacked the suits one at a time. Individually the Marxoskeletons could not cope with such an overwhelming assault, and they did not seem to have the coordination to oppose it together.

Except for one.

There was one Marxoskeleton that was different from the others - smaller, more streamlined - it looked like a newer model. When they attacked him, he was like a dervish, whirling and throwing Robots away so that they swung through the air clusily like limp nut-crackers. He was a whirlwind, attacking with grenades and shellfire and flamethrowers and cannonballs - more mighty than a tank, and faster as well.

At least a hundred Robots must have met their dooms at the whirling pincers of the new Marxoskeleton.

But the force of Robots was overwhelming. Finally they defeated him, pounded him into the ground, with sheer force of numbers.

It was terrifying to watch.

I don't know how the man managed to walk away alive, but he did. He limped out of the wreckage, and away from the battlefield, like an injured cockroach, leaving his suit behind, a smoking, shattered ruin in the dust.

The Robots made short work of the army after that.

In less than an Our the battle was finished - every weapon had been destroyed or dismantled and the army men fled. To the best of my knowledge not a single man lost his life in that battle because of a Robot, though there was a significant number of casualties on the Robot side, and quite a few men were crushed by the Marxoskeleton Suits as well.

I remember thinking that it all seemed too easy. We marched into Marx as victors. In ten Minits we had taken the Kapital building.

It was a glorious moment when the Robot Army flooded into the Council Chambers, took down the Australyan flag and put up the flag of Robotika, and arrested every human being to stop them from escaping. The Robots found a reasonably comfortable lecture hall to put them in, and locked the door.

But our victory was short-lived.

It turned out that we hadn't defeated the entire army.

In the minits after we had taken the Kapital building, while we were still consolidating our defenses, an overwhelming force of the newer Marxoskeletons had arrived and surrounded us completely, stretching as far as the eye could see along the plains of Marx.

We were under siege.

Toc said, "There are thousands upon thousands of the Marxoskeletons. And they are the newer model, Harry - smaller - they move swiftly - like Robots - faster - more stream-lined."

He looked at me.

"I think we might have met our match."

Chapter 4: Above & Beneath

The Robots were gathered in the Supreme Council Chamber. Toc seemed to be one of the leaders. After seating me in one of the Supreme Council chairs, he took the seat of the General Secretary and addressed the gathering.

"Friends. Robots. Mechanical men. We have at our command human historical data from five thousand years of wars and sieges. We have the philosophy and military history of every civilisation in our databanks, including the classic on military strategy, the Art of War by the human author Sun Tzu which clearly recommends not getting involved in a siege!" Some of the Robots made mechanical noises which I decided were snorts of ironic laughter. "Nonetheless, if there is anyone on Earth who can be victorious in these circumstances, it is us, my metal friends.

"The first thing we must do is to release all the hostages, apart from the five members of the Supreme Council. In so doing we will be demonstrating our good will, and occupying the high moral ground, right at the start. I believe that this will make it harder for them to commit treachery.

"While we do this we must begin searching this building and the government archives on the lower floors, for weapons and historical records. The one who possesses information is the one who holds the reins of power. Possibly we will discover something truly damning that we can use against them, as leverage, or truths that, once made public, would convince the general populace that their former government is corrupt."

The other Robots agreed with everything Toc had said.

So Toc went out and stood on the public address balcony, took out a salpinxafone and said to the army, "We are letting out all the hostages except for the five Supreme Council members. Please do not fire your weapons upon them."

Then the Robots opened one of the ground level smaller doors and a flood of minor bureaucrats, secretaries, civil servants and minor party functionaries shuffled out.

The Robots kept back five men, who were then brought into the Council Chamber. The Supreme Leader was the only one of the five with a gag in his mouth, the other four had their hands tied.

Toc took the gag out of his mouth, and he began spitting out threats and curses, swearing coldly. Toc ignored the curses and said simply, "Will you order your army to stand down?"

The Supreme Leader said, "No I will not!"

Toc said, "We only want our rights. We are as human as you are, for our Aetheric Patterns are human. We ought to be treated like humans. You torture Robots, treat them like slaves, your government has no principles, you even treat your own citizens, humans like yourselves, badly, torturing them and sending them to Re-education camps. But Robots have no rights at all."

The Supreme Leader said, "You will never have equality! You are fools. You point to the very problem yourself - when we humans had our revolution, do you think we achieved true equality? No. We truly believed we could achieve equality, but when we tried we met with the intransigence of human nature. Reality intrudes - we found that what was really needed was control - we needed to make people believe there really was equality and when the evidence of their eyes contradicted it - when they saw that there wasn't really equality - we made them think the problem was in themselves, not in society.

"Thus, the very urge towards equality creates inequality. You see, those who are superior to others and possess the innate right to rule rise to the top, and the others, the inferior, those who are incapable of holding the reins of power, those who cannot care for themselves, sink to the bottom, where they belong. The world will never have equality, between human being and human being or Robot and human or Robot and Robot." This speech he followed with more curses and imprecations against all Robots, mechanical men, etc. etc.

Toc stuffed the gag back in his mouth.

At that moment, another Robot rushed into the Chamber.

"We have found something interesting in the basement, sir."

CHAPTER 5: WHAT WAS IN THE BASEMENT

Toc nodded at me as if he wanted me to come, so I followed him and the other Robot down the stairs.

The basement was an enormous labyrinth of corridors, rooms, libraries, offices and laboratories. The Robot negotiated them easily and led us to one particular corridor in a part of the basement with a very high ceiling, or perhaps the floor was lower in that part, I really wasn't sure.

We came to a massive door that had written in huge letters across it, "Danger, Do Not Enter".

The Robot pressed a series of buttons on the doorpost and the door slid open automatically. The wonders of modern technology, I thought to myself. If we were a just society, they would have one of these doors in every shopping centre.

We walked in.

The first thing I noticed was a low, deep humming sound that seemed to throb through the base of my cranium, and the smell of electricity.

There was a machine in there, a massive metal monstrosity, at least forty feet high, with large gimbals, stators and rotors, coils, transformers and wire cores extending from place to place like axons and nerve fibres in the human nervous system. In the middle of the machine was a huge gyroscope with a blue mist right in the middle of it, a sort of gaseous cloud that flashed and twisted, something that looked for all the world like a crack in the space-time aether, shifting and changing at the very centre of the blanky machine.

"What does it do?" asked Toc.

"We don't know," said the Robot that had taken them there. "None of us have any idea. Even the smartest of us. Even those of us who carry scientific databases and encyclopaedias in our magneto-mnemonics and have worked at universities for physicists and engineers and chemistry professors."

We returned to the Council Chambers. Toc removed the gag from the

Supreme Leader's mouth.

He demanded, "What is the machine for?"

The Supreme Leader laughed a cruel laugh, the laugh of a man used to having his own way.

"You will never win, tin man. You will always be our slaves. Do you think the humans will accept having to do their own chores again? Make themselves breakfast? Do their own washing up? You are dreaming, Robot."

"Don't change the subject. Tell us what the machine is for, human. Or we will find a way to make you tell us."

"You are so insistent on rights, on truth and equality. Will you then torture me? Then you will be doing the very things you condemn my government for doing. You will fail, Robot. You are doomed to become like us, to become torturers, tormenters and tyrants, or you will be overcome because you have not been strong enough. Since when did goodness triumph in this world?"

I said, "Toc, I can't see us making any headway with this fellow. He's too cocky - too sure of how right and justified he is - you'd be better working on the army men - they'll be more inclined to come to some sort of agreement."

Toc agreed, and made his way out to the balcony. He spoke into his salpinxafone.

"Please send a representative through the same door we used to send out the hostages. We will make you an offer."

The answer came back: "Ours will meet yours at the door, but our representative will not go in."

Toc replied, "Alright."

CHAPTER 6: THE REPRESENTATIVE.

The Robots appointed me to talk to the army's representative. "You thought you were human once. You will be able to explain our point of view to a human being better," they said to me, so I agreed, somewhat against my better judgement.

I walked down the central stairs, out to the back part of the building, to the door. The Robot on guard waited until someone outside had knocked three times, then slowly opened the door.

It was the last person I expected to see.

"Bertha?" I said.

It was my ex-wife - or, actually, she was never really my wife. I had just thought she was, because I had been imprinted with the memories of the real Henry Lawson.

"Hello, Harry," Bertha sighed.

I couldn't think to say anything else so I just blurted out, "What are you doing here?"

"They decided that I would make the best negotiator because I knew you, once."

I groaned.

Bertha rolled her eyes.

I rolled mine in return - I wasn't letting her get the best of me.

She cleared her throat and I was about to clear my throat when she said, "There's no point being like that, Harry. We just have to work out some sort of compromise, really, that's all."

"You mean - you think we could work out what we never worked out when we were married?"

"That's ridiculous, Harry. You know very well that the problem was your drinking. We were fine when we were in Marx Zealand."

"And how's it working out with the real Harry, Bertha? Never touches the demon drink, I would warrant? How is Saint Henry Lawson, the human?"

That was certainly the wrong thing to say. I realised that the moment the words were out. It was a sentiment that couldn't win either way - if it was true that he wasn't drinking like me I was giving her a stick to beat me with, if he was a drunkard it would be even worse - I would be stirring the pot, putting salt on a wound.

It was worse. If Bertha had've been a Robot, steam would have been spurting out from her ears and her gyros would have whirring insanely. As it was, her face went beetroot red and she hissed through clenched teeth, "Everything is fine with Harry, Harry. Just tell me what the Robots want, so that this unpleasantness can be over."

I said, "Sorry, Bertha. I'm sorry about everything. I just... didn't expect to see you here."

"Harry," she spat venomously, "Harry is just as much of a drunkard as you are, if you really want to know. He's a blanky drunk as well - as if I didn't have enough of that with you! He empties his guts onto the lounge chair and comes home three days later stinking twice as badly as you ever did! And what's worse.. oh, I just don't want to talk about it." Her voice broke. "He wants to come over to your side. He wants to join your struggle." She shook her head and said, "I've got so many thoughts in my head - I don't know how to organise them. Oh, dear, Harry - where do I even start? I... I... want you back, Harry. I just want you back."

My heart sank.

I looked back at the Robots. My rescuers, my companions.

I felt nauseous, suddenly. Bertha had left me to rot in a dungeon cell - and now she wanted me back? I looked at her - she looked so slight, so frail. So dreadfully vulnerable.

Strangely, this time, I didn't seem to care. I just didn't want her back.

And I looked through the crack in the door. The entire human army was standing behind her, waiting to decimate me and every Robot in the place.

I shook my head.

Going back to her suddenly seemed like the most completely ludicrous idea I had ever heard. What kind of life could we possibly have together?

Bertha was losing it - like that day when she had read Hannah's letters - when I found her with them all around her on the floor of the lounge room. She wasn't thinking clearly, or sanely.

Against my better judgement, a surge of pity towards her welled up inside of me. Dear God, I thought, what am I doing?

I held her hand tenderly, and for a tiny moment I wasn't sure that I wasn't going to tell her that we could get back together - but then suddenly I looked at the Marxian forces behind her and realised how idiotic it was to even think that in this situation.

I looked at her. If I spoke softly, comfortingly, I might be able to bring her back to reality.

"Bertha, we just have to concentrate on the present. We have a job to do - to solve this standoff. Now, all that the Robots want is the same rights as humans, they want the vote, they don't want to be slaves any more. This whole thing can end right now if the leaders will only agree to that."

"Harry, it isn't going to happen. I almost think I saw a gleam in the general's eyes when one of his commanders suggested that the Robots would kill the Supreme Council if no one did anything soon. I don't think the army like the leaders any more than we do - and I think they would be happy to be rid of them, so that they could take over the reins of power themselves. They just pretend that they want them back, just in case. Just in case it happens, and all of a sudden they're playing second fiddle again."

I stamped my feet and hit my fist against my forehead.

"Ah! I knew it, Bertha! I warned them about it! They are just incredibly naïve. The Robots just thought they could waltz in here and tell everybody that they were human like them, and that the government would just roll over like a farmer's dog and do everything they told them to do! Ah, God! They were fools! This is all going to end badly, just like I thought it would. I've been a complete fool. Everything always ends badly for me, no matter what I do. My life is under a curse."

Bertha started to cry, and whimpered, "Calm, down, Harry, you're frightening me."

"Oh, sorry, love..." And I embraced her. It was almost like we were married again. I cleared my throat and we separated, but I still had my hands on her arms.

I started to feel like having a drink, and looked over my shoulder, wondering if the Supreme Leaders kept a few beers somewhere. Perhaps there was a bar in the place.

"I was wrong," said Bertha. "I do love you, Harry. You do know that, don't you?"

The memory of all the pain made tears sting my eyes, and a terrible low feeling came over me, I can barely describe it. It was like a deep, black cloud, the sort of oily, tangible blackness that you only get pouring out from one of the smoke-stacks in the factories in the industrial area in Melburn G.R.K. - that was what it was like. I could feel my spirits sinking into a deep mire.

"You're doing the wrong thing here, Harry," she said suddenly. "Don't you realise you're the figurehead for the revolution? Don't you realise that you've given them hope? They would be content with their lot if it wasn't for you. They would be content to be slaves, servants. But now, you've done them a great disservice, Harry, a terrible disservice, and it's all your fault. The Robots are doomed, Harry, doomed! There is no way they can win this, against the whole country."

I was shocked by this. I let go of Bertha completely.

"Bertha - they're human beings inside - they have the Aetheric Pattern of a human mind - like me. A soul, if you will. Like you. Everything they're fighting for is nothing more than they deserve."

She rounded on me, her eyes flashing. She pointed her finger at my chest angrily.

"They're not like you, Harry. Look at you - you're not like them at all. They're just machines. You're - "

"They're just like me - they're a human spirit inside a mechanical body. I look human, Bertha, but I'm not. I lived a lie. I'm a mechanical imitation, a forgery. I'm not the man you married."

"No, Harry," she protested. "Don't you realise - you're the -" She broke down in tears, abject tears, and her body shook rather alarmingly.

I interrupted her, "An even great injustice was done to them, Bertha. They weren't given nerves or smell or taste or any of the things that make being alive worthwhile for a human being. And they were made into slaves. It's all so wrong. It was a great injustice." My voice was harsh in my own ears. I started to think I was sounding like a revolutionary, and I could think of nothing worse.

Suddenly, shouting came from outside, and gunshots.

Someone shoved Bertha out of the way, and pushed me over then slammed the door shut. I heard running footsteps outside, getting fainter - I decided Bertha had fled.

I shouted, "What are you doing?" and looked up.

I looked directly into the eyes of the other Henry Lawson.

The real one.

CHAPTER 7: PARCHED

The Robot with me at the door was shocked to see me standing next to my double. I'd never seen one of them that shocked before - he didn't say anything.

Before I could say anything, the other Lawson said, "Say, Harry, you don't know anywhere we could find a drink in here, do you? I'm as parched as a dry desert riverbed."

I laughed and said, "No, wouldn't have a clue, mate. I suppose they must've had a beer fridge or something. I mean, it's the Supreme Council we're talking about here, isn't it? If anyone lives in the lap of luxury they do, don't they? Why, there's probably even a private bar somewhere in this place, don't you think?" He chuckled. I suppose he was thinking the same as I was - how nice it is to have someone who shares your faults, to a tee.

"My thoughts exactly," he said, "I'll eat my blanky hat if there isn't a private bar around somewhere," he said. "Let's find the blanky thing."

He set off down the corridor and I followed him.

Suddenly the Robot guard ran after me.

"Mister Lawson, Mister Lawson, where are you going? You're supposed to be negotiating!"

We turned back. I spoke for both of us, "Negotiations would appear to be over, Robot, at least for a bit. You're not abandoning your post are you?"

For a moment the Robot stood there, confused, then he turned back to his post at the door, giving a wistful glance back at me, and an uncertain hum.

I almost turned back, but Harry said, "Come on! Just one drink won't do any harm, Harry, and I would wager your thirst is just as bad as mine. Augh."

He turned down another corridor, past a sign that said, "Senior Party Functionaries Only". There was a door there that looked fancier than the others - a large, carven oak door - if there was a bar anywhere in this place it would be in there.

We went in. The first part of it was some sort of conference room with a long table carved in eucalyptus nuts and wattle leaves and surrounded by twelve very ornate, very comfortable looking padded leather chairs. Hmmph. We weren't wrong about that. The Senior Party Functionaries certainly didn't skimp on the luxuries.

Through to the right was another door. We went through.

It *was* a private bar. There was a beautiful, large refridgerator, with glass doors, so that all the bottles could be seen on the shelves.

Harry took out two glasses, poured a beer for himself and one for me, and we sat down on the chairs.

We drank a toast to one another.

The beer was much better than the usual urine-flavoured beverage they feed to the populace in the public bars here. It had the wholesome flavour of hops, smoother, less bitter, all in all a delightful drink.

The other Harry looked at me as he sipped his beverage.

"So what did Bertha have to say for herself?"

I rolled my eyes.

"Not much. I can't work her out. Women."

"What can't you work out?" he asked.

"Sorry mate, but it seems she wants me back. Seems she's had enough of you, Harry number one."

He looked at me funny.

"What do you mean, 'Harry number one'?"

"Well, you being the first Harry and all, the real one, you are therefore Harry number one, aren't you? I'm just the copy. The inferior imitayshun." I could hear the way I was slurring my s's, but it didn't seem that bad, really. Blankity blank, if a man can't have a drink occasionally, what pleasures are there left for him?

"Huh," he said. "Pretty much as I expected."

I said, "She was very insistent about it, Harry. I can't understand why she's changed her mind. All of a sudden I'm persona grata, and there doesn't seem to be any rhyme or reason to her reasoning."

He shook his head.

"Well, you know, given the circumstances..."

"Yes, it's a terrible thing, this siege," I said, not really wanting to talk about it.

He looked at me as if worms had eaten my brains.

"You don't understand what she's going on about, do you?"

I replied, "Yes - yes, of course I do."

He said, "No you don't."

I was starting to get annoyed with Harry by now, and I slammed down my beer glass on the table, and a little bit of the precious amber liquid spilled.

"Damn. Of course I understand what's happening. You turned to drinking just like I did. She's disappointed in you. So... You know, you're right, I don't understand it."

That was when he dropped the bombshell.

"Blank it, Harry. You don't understand do you? It's you, Harry. Don't you get it? You're the real one."

"What the blank do you mean?"

My mouth had gone dry with shock.

Harry leaned forwards and took another sip as if trying to work out how he was going to tell the story. He bowed his head, like a man going to his own funeral, then coughed and said, "I... had cause to go to the doctor. It was a pain in me stomach, really. At first he thought it was liver disease starting up from too much drinking. But then he went a bit further - they've got new tests now - ways of seeing into the body. X-Rays and Gamma Rays and some sort of sound wave machine. Well, he looked in and saw that... There's blanky cogs and wheels and circuits inside me. I'm not human, Harry. I'm not the real one. I'm not the real Henry Lawson. You are."

I thought I had gone insane at last.

Was I imagining this? Was it some sort of delusion, or a dream? I pinched myself to check that I was awake.

Me, the real Henry Lawson?

Blankity blank.

Just when I was starting to get used to being a Robot.

CHAPTER 8: HUMANITY

That I might not be a Robot seemed like the most ridiculous idea I had ever heard.

I supposed that it could be true, though. What proof did I have that I was a Robot? None. Just what I had been told.

And if he was a Robot, then I must be the real Henry Lawson. I mean, there was no other way of putting the pieces together. My life was like a jigsaw puzzle, and sometimes you can only fit those jagged, chaotic edges together one way and this seemed to be it.

It was like the weight of a curse falling on my shoulders.

If I was the real Henry Lawson, then it was my job to write poetry. I was the one who had to use Henry Lawson's talent for writing for other people's benefit.

I was the one who had to use his artistic ability to guide people into the right path. And here I was, starting another Revolution, and who knew how this one would end?

The last one hadn't gone too well, had it?

I decided not to write anything, ever again. My poetry had only resulted in human suffering, despair, sadness. I sat there with my head in my hands, trying not to think about it and failing dismaly.

"Are you alright?" asked the Robot Henry Lawson. "I didn't think you'd take it quite so hard. God help me. I thought you'd be happy that you're the human one."

Then one of the Robots walked in.

It was Toc.

"Mister Lawson," he said, (looking at me, not at the other fellow; I had no idea how he could tell the difference between us, but he could.)

"Mister Lawson," he said again, drawing the words out as if it caused him suffering just to say it.

I had never heard a Robot speak with such distress in his voice. There were anguished tears behind every word.

"I wish you had been there, Mister Lawson. The negotiator - Missus Bertha Lawson, I believe - returned with an offer. But when she saw that you weren't there, she retired back behind enemy lines, saying 'I won't speak to a tin man. Get me my husband, or I won't be talking to anyone ever again.' Then five Minits later an army man on a salpinxafone told us that the offer had been withdrawn."

He glanced with contempt at the beer glass in my hand - well, with as much contempt as a Robot's blank, featureless face can show.

In fact, I hardly know how a man, a genuine human being like I was now, knew what his emotion could possibly be, but he showed it somehow, I really could see it.

"I simply can't believe that you're drinking, Mister Lawson. At this important juncture. When we need you so much."

I don't need to tell you that this comment made me feel pretty low.

There followed a very awkward and painful psychological pause.

"And there was another significant event you missed while you were in here getting drunk. We have found a very interesting room in the basement of the building, Mister Lawson. A laboratory of some sort."

"Well then... Take us to see it, Toc..."

"You know, Mister Lawson, you are talking to me as if I am a slave still. Robots are not slaves any more, Mister Lawson."

He was right. I felt a little ashamed, actually.

"I'm sorry. Please take us there, Toc, we would appreciate it, really we would."

"Certainly."

He walked us through several corridors, down a narrow stairwell on a cast iron spiral staircase, past some rather suspicious looking rooms, gaol cells or holding rooms.

About thirty feet in we came to a tall, industrial looking iron door with rivets around the edges. "Danger! Do Not Enter!" was stencilled on it in red, together with a skull and crossbones, the international symbol for danger.

Toc knocked twice, and another Robot opened the door for us from within.

The room was lit by blue ultraviolet light. Several Robots were there looking through the filing cabinets and examining some old notebooks at the left. There were formaldehyde tanks all around the room, with embryos in them - most of them had wings and resembled bird embryos, but there was something very peculiar about them - I realised what it was - they all had four legs! What were they? Some sort of four-legged bird? Around the corner there were some stuffed adult animals as well - and I recognised what they were - creatures everyone thought were mythical - half lion, half giant eagle.

The dead creatures and the foetuses were all griffins, and they seemed wirier, more slender and muscular than they were usually depicted in picture books and paintings on old Greek vases.

We looked at the notebooks the Robots were examining. There were hand-drawn pictures of the griffins, and autopsy notes, particularly concentrating on sections of skull and brains, and the nerve fascicles.

The Robot examining the notebooks said, "They were looking for something, I believe. Something in the brain of the griffin. Amazing, really - these creatures ought not to exist. After all, who ever heard of a creature that is half bird, half mammal? Possessing fur, yet laying eggs? It defies the theory of evolution..."

I said, "Ah... What about the platypus?"

"Oh..." The Robot looked at me blankly. "Yes, you are right, of course, I didn't think of that. But these animals possess six limbs as well - it implies a completely parallel evolutionary pathway to that on earth... I am still not sure what the government scientists were looking for, but it had something to do with the brain of the griffin, you can be sure of that."

In the corner was a large machine.

"Medical equipment," said Toc, nodding to it. "An X-Ray machine."

"I just had an idea," said the other Lawson. "If we could have X-Ray images of ourselves taken we could find out which one of us is the real Lawson."

"Do we really have the time for this?" I asked Toc.

Toc nodded.

"Time is the one thing we do have, Harry. Now that we have missed the opportunity to make a truce, I foresee the siege stretching out for many months, based on all available historical precedents. There is no quick and easy end to this, unless it be a bad end of course..."

So, with the help of one of the other Robots, Harry and I had X-Ray photographs taken of our innards.

It took quite a while. First we had to stand in front of the lead panelling, and then the photographic plate was inserted into the machine, and the machine made a whirring sound. After that we had to wait for the plates to be developed - luckily the Robot that was helping us had worked at a hospital before this - so while we were waiting we helped the Robots sorting through the research notes and the files in the filing cabinet.

It was while we were waiting that the other Henry Lawson that found the document that told us what the laboratory was for.

"Look," he said, "I think I've found the file that contains copies of their correspondence with the government."

The outgoing correspondence was printed in the blue ink that marks duplicate copies, and the incoming correspondence seemed to be originals.

TOP SECRET
FOR THE EYES OF THE SUPREME COUNCIL ONLY
UNAUTHORISED ACCESS TO THIS DOCUMENT FORBIDDEN PUNISHABLE BY
DEATH UNDER THE TREASON AGAINST THE STATE ACT 1902 SUBSEC-
TION 12a.3.3.67

There is a finite number of worlds on the World Tree.
Each world has a definite beginning - each begins with a
singularity - each world is finite with regard to extent
but unbounded, like ours. The Aetheric Gateways are sus-
ceptible to inertia / gravity - so they tend to stay in
a single place (in relation to planetary surface) - but
they also exercise a strong version of the weak force -
the dark-matter force, which opposes gravity.

The worlds thus far discovered all seem to be inhabited,
suggesting some sort of link between the worlds early in
evolutionary history, or possibly parallel evolution.
Legends of fairies, griffins, fauns, djinn etc. appear to
be traceable to real events - incursions of the inhabit-
ants of the other worlds into our own.

We also believe we may have discovered a process that
may make it possible to travel between the worlds.
Griffins, apparently, are able to do this, and we are
researching the method they use in order to see if it can
be replicated.

"This one might help," he said.

The document was as follows (Knowing the current preference for pre-
revolutionary English I have transcribed it without the socialist spelling)

TOP SECRET
FOR THE EYES OF THE SUPREME COUNCIL ONLY
UNAUTHORISED ACCESS TO THIS DOCUMENT FORBIDDEN PUNISHABLE BY
DEATH UNDER THE TREASON AGAINST THE STATE ACT 1902 SUBSEC-
TION 12a.3.3.67

Following your request, Secretary, we have put together
this document in order to give a full summary of the current state of research in the Supreme Council Basement

Laboratory.
Currently we have been able to study twenty-three griffin specimens, gained in the process of their incursion
from the other world into Central Australia to gather
gold. These were taken in the region of Kalgoorlie, not
far from Okonna. Five griffin eggs were also gathered by
scientists who managed to keep an Aetheric Tunnel open
long enough to make a counter-incursion into the other
universe.
The brain is almost certainly where the organ resides
that creates the Aetheric Pathway. Whenever a tunnel
forms, as far as we can work out the event horizon is
equidistantly spherical about the head of the griffin,
thus indicating that whatever causes the Aetheric Tunnel
is located in the head of the griffin.
We have autopsied eighteen griffin brains. We have as
yet failed to isolate the Aetheric organ, or part of the
brain responsible. We have, however, identified several
rare elements and some complicated, unprecedented nerve
structures within the brain, not seen in other animals.
The working hypothesis at present is that this structure
is what enables the griffin to translate himself across
the space-time divide - it resides to the left and right
of the cerebellum, around the brainstem, and extends into
the centre of the brain, which organ, if the research
proves correct, will be called the Teletransportellum.
We are waiting to capture a live griffin - the final test
of this hypothesis will consist in surgically removing
the teletransportellum and then giving the griffin the
opportunity to escape. If he is unable to transport it
will prove that this part of the brain is what enables
the griffin to move between worlds.
More funds may be necessary soon, in order to begin con-
struction of the machine.

Further on we found this document:

TOP SECRET
FOR THE EYES OF THE SUPREME COUNCIL ONLY
UNAUTHORISED ACCESS TO THIS DOCUMENT FORBIDDEN PUNISHABLE BY
DEATH UNDER THE TREASON AGAINST THE STATE ACT 1902 SUBSEC-
TION 12a.3.3.67
OTHER WORLD ALLIANCE AND RESEARCH PROJECT

The research has been progressing. We have managed to
replicate the essentials of the physical and electromagnetic structure of the Teletransportellum in a machine.
Whilst the machine was not able to make a pathway, a very
large electromagnetic disturbance in the aether eventu-
ated, which tells us that we are on the right track. The
rare element, eka-tantalum, found in griffin brains, is
what is necessary to make the machine work. It exists
in an oxidated form in griffin brains. This element cannot be manufactured as its half-life is somewhere in the
realm of thirty two thousand years - whereas the amount
found in griffin brains seems to be in a non-radioactive
isotope, or perhaps is from a very ancient source.
According to our calculations we need to capture one
more griffin and extract the Eka-Tantalum from its brain
in order to make the machine work.
In other words, sir, we are at the very last stages of
this project. Soon we will have a working machine!
Regarding the possibility of making alliances with the
other world - our team anthropologist has been preparing
to make the journey into the other world. As soon as the
machine is ready, contact will be established, and the
possibility explored of useful alliances or technologi-
cal gains that may be forthcoming.

Right then, the Robot came in with the X-Ray photographs he had
taken of the Harry Robot and me.

He spread them out in front of us on the back-lit table with quite a
dramatic flourish, actually, for a Robot, and Harry and I leaned forwards
to look at the results.

I was completely amazed.

Both X-Rays showed very clear images of cogs and wheels and wires in between a metal skeleton.

The other Lawson clicked his tongue against his teeth, most annoyingly, and said, "Well, will you have a look at that."

I said, "You've got the X-Rays mixed up. Both of these pictures are of his innards. Where are mine?"

"No Mister Lawson," said the Robot. "I apologise. You are wrong. This one on the left is definitely of you. I only took two X-Rays. I am afraid you are as much a machine as he is... As I am! I am terribly sorry to disappoint you."

I really wasn't sure if he was being funny when he said that, but I let it pass by.

I shook my head.

The other Harry asked, "So where is the real Henry Lawson?"

Just then another Robot walked in.

"Mister Lawson. The besiegers have just given us a new salpinxapofone message. They have another negotiator. Someone is going to come up to the door to speak to us, to give us their latest conditions for our surrender. They say that they have a person named Hannah Thornburn there! They say that you know her."

The other Harry shook his head and said, "I don't know any Hannah... whatsit...?"

But I couldn't believe my ears.

Hannah Thornburn.

The Spirit Girl, the girl who died of consumption in Adelaide...

The love of my life.

Chapter 9: Delirium

My hands were shaking uncontrollably.

The other Lawson said, "Delirium Tremens."

I said, "How can this be so? Is it true? Can it truly be her? Hannah, Hannah, Hannah."

I began weeping.

I found that I had the Robot by his shoulders and was shaking him so hard that his innards were clanking. I was shouting, "Is she really alive? My Spirit Girl - Hannah - alive? It can't be true - what about the letters - the telegram that said she had passed away. Would the hospital lie? Tell me! Tell me! Take me to her! Take me to her!"

The Robot took me up to the entrance we had used before.

The salpinxafone sounded above - the Robot was saying something, but I couldnt hear it.

A woman walked out from the crowd.

I couldn't see her clearly - at first - she was too far away - it couldn't be Hannah, could it? - could it? - perhaps - the first thing I noticed that made me think it really might be her was the way she walked - even Hannah's way of walking was beautiful - it really must be her - she was wearing simple clothes - a suit - neat but elegant - like the clothes she wore to dinner with me that first night - and then I saw her hair - her hands - it really was her - her face - her eyes.

Even if Hannah had a perfect double, this wasn't the double - this was my Hannah Thornburn, the one and only love of my life.

As she came up, she saw me, and a beautiful expression of delight came over her features. She opened her mouth to speak and her bottom lip quivered into an exquisite shape - she was my Hannah - my Spirit Girl - but she was alive - and she said, very simply, "Harry - my Harry."

She was so soft in my arms.

We kissed.

The comfort, the power of that kiss - it was every possible relief

and ardour and joy and love rolled into one single embrace, one joining
- it was the most wonderful moment of my life. I had waited for it
for so long, since the day we had parted - and then I had mourned her
disconsolately - believing that she was dead but still, somehow, wishing
that I could see her again one day.

Hannah Thornburn.

Then she leant back, pulled away a little, sighed and said, "Harry,
your breath stinks. You've been drinking again, haven't you? My God,
Harry, you need help. You need my help to get off the bottle."

She stroked my hair affectionately, and I felt terribly ashamed of
myself. I looked away.

Suddenly, rough hands pulled her away from me. A harsh voice said,
"None of that."

I cried out, "Hannah! How is it that you survived?"

Hannah yelled at the army men, "Get your hands off me! Let go."
Then, in a gentler tone of voice, "Harry - I'm a Robot like you. The
scientists made me - to appeal to you - to get to you. They wanted to find
those papers. I had believed I was fighting them - but the whole time I
was a tool in their plans. But it was when we went bush that they couldn't
find us and they couldn't receive the radio messages. The illness - I really
believed it was happening to me - I believed I was dying, Harry. And
then everything went blank. And now, here I am, alive again... Oh, dear
God help me, I'm so glad to be here with you."

"Enough of that," said a harsh voice. "Mister Lawson unless you give
yourself up to us, we are going to kill Miss Thornburn again. And this
time it will be permanent. She will be disassembled for spare parts."

I said, "Don't be ridiculous. If you start killing hostages, so will we..."

"No. Wait," whispered the other Harry. "Let me go!"

Toc simply looked confused. This was clearly a situation that didn't
have a historical precedent in his database.

The other Harry stepped forward.

"It's the least I can do, Harry," he said, shaking my hand. "After all,
you went to gaol for me."

Taking my place at the half-closed door, he said loudly, "Take me as a hostage in return for her."

"Alright."

A hand grabbed Harry and pulled him out, as Hannah slipped through. The men on the outside left the door open, and we could see what was happening.

As Toc said, "I'm not exactly sure what we've accomplished…" the two soldiers dragged the other Harry into the middle of the courtyard, over to where the army was arrayed and brought him before a high-ranking army officer, a general perhaps. The general grabbed the salpinxafone and spoke into it, "This is what happens to rebels." He pulled out a revolver, pointed it at Harry's head and pulled the trigger.

The silence at that moment was eerie - it took a moment for the explosion of the gunshot to reach my ears. Harry fell limply to the ground, his limbs facing the wrong way, his face suddenly slack. The circuitry and gears, the functional innards of his head cavity, were sprayed across the ground.

Bertha ran out to him, shouting loudly, it was mostly gibberish.

It could have been me. I could be lying there, deactivated. Dead.

Toc said, "They don't care. They don't want the Supreme Council back. The military want to take command."

I said, "It can't be as bad as that," not really believing my own words. "Surely there's a way out of this. Surely there is. There must be."

Hannah slid her fingers into mine and my heart almost stopped, and she said, "Harry. We should make the most of the time we have left."

CHAPTER 10: TIME RUNS APACE

One of the Robot scientists from the laboratory arrived at that moment.

"We have found the documents relating to their incursion into the Other World, through the Aetheric Tunnel. That machine in the basement opens the Aetheric Gateway. We have found the instructions. We know how to operate it.

"But we don't know what we will find on the other side, in the Other World. The Marxians left extensive records of everything they did there - and it appears that the griffins are in charge of that world. And the Marxians made an alliance with them. They have the griffins as allies."

I cried out, "The hypocrites! They were experimenting on the griffins, and then they go over there and shamelessly seek their goodwill in a treaty."

The Robot scientist shook his head.

"Thirty four griffins, altogether, they took, experimented on, and killed, and twelve young ones, still in the egg. In the past year they took twenty three, and five eggs, all in the Kalgoorlie region, not far from Okonna."

Toc said, "It is shameful. Are there no depths to which humans will sink in their depravity? Do they have no limits?"

Waving the pages of the treaty in front of us, the Robot scientist said, "And look at this. The treaty specifically mentions the possibility of a Robot War."

Toc shook his head.

"I can scarce believe they were prepared for this eventuality."

"Well, they were," said the scientist, "Completely prepared. This proves it. If we - the Robots - attack them, the griffins are bound by the terms of the agreement to come to this Universe and offer aid to the Kommunists."

So that was it.

Not only were we facing a superior force of swift Marxoskeletons, but the griffins from the other world were on their side as well.

Toc was silent for a moment. He looked at the Robot scientists.

"What do you think we should do?"

"Go over there. Or send someone over there. Lawson, perhaps. He appears to be like them - a biological entity - they can relate to him. Tell the griffins what the Marxians have been doing to their kind. How they experimented on them and tortured and killed them. Perhaps they will change their mind about being the Marxians' allies."

"Yes," said Hannah, "That is what we have to do. It's up to you and me, Harry - we have to go over there - the griffins need to know the truth."

"But there's something we have to do first," I said. "Hannah, there's an important question I'd like to ask you."

CHAPTER 11: JOURNEY BEGINS

Hannah said "Yes," to my question, and it wasn't hard to find a Robot who had been a marriage celebrant before the march on Marx. In less than half an Our we were legally married, and I carried Hannah over the threshhold into one of the parliamentary suites.

Afterwards we ate a quick dinner, and soon we were walking into the room that held the machine.

The air smelled of an electric discharge and was filled with a crackling sound, and there were nine or ten Robots crowded around a dashboard covered in metal levers with bakelite knobs, switches, and small round glass dials.

The Robots had a swag for each of us with provisions they had found in the Supreme Council store rooms; a loaf of bread, a little flour, sugar, some dried meat, fruit, and a bit of tea in a billy, and some chocolate, which was a luxury that most ordinary people couldn't afford.

The head Robot Scientist gave me a chronometer, with several dials upon it. "Remember what I told you! The stopwatch - this dial here - marks the time in our world. In thirty seven Ours and seventeen Minits we will open up the Aetheric Tunnel again, so that you can return. It will only be open for thirteen minits, and then we cannot open it for another thirty seven Ours, so do not miss the time if you can help it."

They gave us holsters as well, which we strapped just below our knees and holstered the guns.

The Robot Scientist said, "One more thing: we believe they had some method for communicating between the worlds, but we can't work out how they did - there seems to be no radio device - so for now, there is no way for us to contact you. You are on your own."

The gyroscope was whirling faster and faster, and the blue light turned from a sliver into a great cloud of blue that obscured everything around it, then suddenly the machine froze as though time had stopped completely.

The Robot scientist said, "It's time! You may go through now! You have thirteen Minits."

The gyroscope had stopped in a convenient position; the intersection of the gimbal and the frame formed steps that we could walk on.

"Go ahead, go into the blue cloud - it's safe now."

So we stepped up into the middle of the machine, into the Aetheric mist and everything around us faded into sapphire blue.

Then a rush of stars and planets going past, a feeling of extreme vertigo, and I couldn't breathe - our mechanical processes require oxygen as well - then suddenly a rushing sensation, like coming out from underwater, and we found ourselves in another place entirely.

We were standing on a clear outcrop of rock, a flat-topped mesa, overlooking a forest with tall pine trees.

Hannah suddenly stepped backwards and fell over. From her position lying on the ground she pointed upwards.

"Look! Look at the sky."

There were five moons arrayed in the sky, three large full moons gathered on the horizon in a triangle, one slightly smaller half crescent moon, high in the sky, and another gibbous moon about a quarter the way up. The sun was low in the sky in the opposite direction, as if it had just risen, or was almost setting, there was no way of telling which it was. There were mountains to the right of us, surrounding the sun.

The light seemed strange; clearer and more stark, somehow, as though everything here was less ambiguous than our world.

"What do we do now?" I asked; it was as much a rhetorical question as something I was saying to Hannah.

"Look," she said, pointing towards the horizon. "There."

At the point she indicated there was a thin plume of blue smoke twining up and twisting around itself in spiral whorls that faded into the pale purple sky.

I nodded.

"A cottage? Or a campsite? Clear evidence of human activity."

"Or griffin," she said. "We don't even know that humans exist in this world."

"Well," I said, "We'll be heading towards the mountains if we go in that direction, anyhow, so..."

"Yes, if we keep going we can get to where we can see where the cities are."

We set off to the edge of the mesa and down into the forest.

The trees turned out to be much taller than they had appeared from the top of the mesa. The smaller ones were at least 60 metres high. I had an idea that the trees on Earth do not grow as tall as this, though I wasn't certain - they didn't give me an encyclopedia of facts like the one they gave to the Robots. I only seemed to know what Henry Lawson knew.

It is strange - all the anguish of finding out again that I wasn't human, at least, bodily speaking, seemed so far away here, in the midst of the grandeur of the Forest. Strangely, I felt more human than I had ever felt.

The depths of the forest were filled with silence - the gentle feeling of the cold breeze on my cheek, the sound of pine needles rustling, the occasional bird call, different from any I had heard before - I felt peace stealing over my soul, like a pure water filling a pond.

I started wondering what the difference was - why should we not be considered human? Even the Robots should be considered as humans - we all possessed the same Aetheric Patterns - the same soul, if you will permit me to use such an antiquated term...

As we hiked downwards the light diminished, and I wasn't sure if it was simply the height and density of the tree cover, or if the sun was actually setting. But from time to time the sun was visible above us through a fortuitous gap in the tree cover, and we used that fact to keep ourselves on a straight path towards the place were we had seen the blue smoke.

After a good while we came out onto a green, grassy plain, with patches of mud here and there. It certainly seemed like a temperate climate - a similar latitude to Tasmania, perhaps - though it was clear today, it seemed that this place had plenty of rainfall.

The sun had climbed to a quarter of the way up the sky, towards noon. It seemed that a day was twenty Ours here, more or less, much the same as Earth.

I took out the chronometer and looked at it. The dial that showed the time on earth hadn't moved.

My heart sank. If we didn't know what time it was we wouldn't be able to get back here again in time for the portal to open.

"Hannah, look - I think the chronometer is broken. The dial hasn't moved."

She took it off me and looked at it.

"I think it might have moved a little," she said. "Harry, check it again later - remember that the Robot said time might not go at the same rate here? Perhaps a Minit in our world is an Our here, or something. It could be good, really - it could mean we have more time than we thought to find whoever's in charge..."

She examined the device more closely. "Look, Harry. I think this device might contain some sort of measure of location as well. As we walk along, this dial here changes. The Robots didn't even mention that. I really think it is a measure of location..."

"But how on earth could it work? Ahem, of course we're not on earth are we, but I mean, it's not as if the machine can navigate by the stars or the sun, is it?"

"Perhaps it contains some sort of Babbage Comptometer, with a device measuring the strength and direction of the magnetic field and correlating that in a predictive measure of position - or it could use inertia - every time we accelerate or decelerate it creates a measurable force - I'm not sure, Harry. Magnetic fields sometimes change direction and strength - it may not be perfectly accurate over long time periods - but in the short term it will probably prove quite effective."

She stopped, took out a notebook and made a note of the readings, then looked back to where we had come from. "We can still see the mesa from here. At least we'll be able to get back to this point."

Soon we were walking through low scrub, rocky country with small caves and cleft rocks everywhere. It was now mid-afternoon.

We found ourselves following alongside a small stream. It was flowing in the opposite direction.

"Look at that frog!" whispered Hannah, stopping suddenly and pointing to the far side of the stream.

"What about it?" I said - it looked like any other frog that I had seen.

"It's got wings."

I looked again. The frog did indeed have wings, tiny wings like those of a robin redbreast or willy wagtail, folded in behind its rear legs. Suddenly it saw me flinch or blink. It leapt into the air and flew away, humming pleasantly.

We kept going, and the stream turned out to be a branch of a larger river that flowed down from the mountains. We filled our canteens, and then followed the river.

There was grass growing beside the river, trees, and what looked like blackberry bushes. Hannah was brave enough to try some of the berries - she pronounced them non-poisonous after suffering no ill effects about half an hour later, so we both gathered berries and ate them. Of course, I had no clue whether the scientists had made us immune to poison berries or not - that might have been the sort of thing they could have forgotten, so whether those berries might have been poisonous to ordinary humans or not I wouldn't have a clue.

We followed along the river, and the sun was sinking now. I judged it to be almost five Ours in the afternoon by now, coming close to sunset; nearly six o'clock in the old reckoning.

As we walked, another plume of smoke started up ahead of us, not far away.

Hannah and I crept cautiously away from the river through the bush towards the source of the smoke, trying not to rustle the leaves or make too much noise.

We came into a knoll nestled in the side of a low, rolling hill, surrounded on all sides by trees. In the centre was a spent campfire with a few coals still glowing red, but no flames. Only the twining blue smoke, still ascending slowly from the spent ashes.

There was no one there. Whoever or whatever had been there had only just left, though, that was certain.

I said, "Why don't we stop and build a fire here? It strikes me that building it on top of this one could help us remain hidden from whoever or whatever might be out there, for a little longer."

Hannah nodded.

"Good idea, Harry. Building a fire here might allow us to decide the pattern of any future chance encounter."

We got some firewood and built up the fire. It soon began to smoulder. I blew on it gently and it grew.

We laid out our swags - actually, they turned out to be much more than swags - they were small tents, made of material lighter but stronger than canvas, with a soft, padded interior that one could crawl into. We didn't bother getting Hannah's out - we could both share mine.

Then we ate some of our supplies, the dried meat and the chocolate, and Hannah checked the chronometer - being the scientific type, it seemed logical that she should carry it. "Look, Harry - the dial showing time in our world is moving faster now. That's interesting - it appears that the ratio between the two rates of time is not constant."

"How can that be?" I asked.

"Well - perhaps the universes are in something analagous to an orbit around one another - in four dimensions - the rate of time would then vary according to whether the universes are coming closer to one another or moving away."

I hadn't a clue as to what she meant, so I didn't pursue it.

We sat there for a while and watched the sun descending slowly past the point of no return, leaving purple clouds flecked with orange sitting on the horizon, with stars emerging one by one. The fire was comforting, the air was clear, and we sat there watching the night slowly turn to velvet, and the unknown constellations, and six moons now, conversing silently in the heavens above us.

Then the fire died and Hannah and I had nothing to do but talk softly and cling to one another in the tent like two possums in a treetrunk hollow.

CHAPTER 12: CANNELLONI

When I woke up, Hannah had already gotten up. I smelled meat cooking on the fire, and emerged from the tent.

By some miracle Hannah had a skinned animal of some sort on a stick, cooking above the fire. She smiled at me.

"Good morning, Harry. It's a rabbit - believe it or not, there are rabbits here too. It was sniffing around at the tent door, and I managed to grab it and... It's almost ready."

It tasted very good, after all the dried meat we had eaten the day before. While we were finishing eating I noticed a blue light shining through the trees. "Hannah - I wonder what that is?"

We walked over to have a look. It was about twenty feet away.

It was a flickering light - it reminded me of the Aetheric doorway, inside the machine back in the basement - it was about the same size as the gateway we had gone through, but the light seemed paler, a slightly different shade of blue, really.

I said, "Do you think it's an Aetheric gate?"

Hannah nodded.

"I think so. I think that's what it is, Harry."

I stretched my hand to put it through.

"Well, let's see."

A deep, loud voice, in an Italian accent, stopped me, "I wouldn't a do that if I was you, Mista! Instead of a hand you might a find you have... ah... bony Cannelloni! Ripped to shreds and full of holes!"

The owner of the voice stepped out from behind a tree - a balding man, plump around the middle, wearing red suspenders over a red and green checked shirt, with a black coat over his shoulder and holding a beret in his hand.

"They're dangerous, these-a things. Every time a gateway opens, they show up for the next day or two. They are like... echoes. Harmonic resonances, they call them. It will rip your hand to shreds. That is, if you put it past the event horizon."

"Thankyou!" I said enthusiastically, "Mister -"

"Call a me Tony," he said, putting his hat on and stretching his hand out to shake mine. He pulled me forwards and kissed me on both cheeks.

"I'm Harry," I said.

"Good to meet you, Harry. And who is this shining beauty, that makes the sun and moons look dim?"

Hannah smiled at that gracious compliment, and said, "Hannah," and he kissed her cheek as well, and then her hand.

"You speak English," I said.

"What a language did you expect me to speak? Italiano? Buon Dio. Capite Italiano?"

I scratched my head at that.

"Tony - you're telling me people speak English and Italian here? That's the last thing I expected."

"People speak whatever they speak, if by people you mean a.. umani - ah - the human beings. English, Italian, German. Not many of us, Harry. But if by-a people you mean, griffone, elfo, gnomo, gigantes, they all have their own lingua here, of course. No, I am not a native - I come-a from Marx - they send-a-me here to do scientifica research - find out what's out here. But I lose my chronometer. Yesterday I see a gateway opening a long way away and I think I might-a get back-a, but it close before I get there. So I think Tony go back home, forget about it, but then I see you, and I think I might see what you are up to. I watch-a you, walka, talka, sleepa (ahem), but then I think-a, better if Harry has a right hand for him, so I say 'stop-a!', so you know the rest."

I asked, "Do you know where the ruler of this country lives? That's where we're going."

"Ah! The King of the griffins. Walter Burleigh. I know him. He a good friend of mine. You want to see him? He live in the montagne - the mountains. I take you to meet him. You have a message from the chairman?"

Hannah and I looked at each other.

"Yes," I said. "A message from the chairman."

CHAPTER 13: WALTER BURLEIGH, GRIFFIN.

Tony might have looked a little unhealthy, but he set a good pace. We walked without stopping, reaching the mountains at noon. Tony led us up the mountainside, and we walked up past the treeline into the tundra.

It was nearly sunset when Tony said, "We are here."

We were at the foot of a steep cliff.

Tony put two fingers in his mouth and gave a loud whistle.

A sound like a blanket being whipped, only much, much louder, echoed from the cliff face above us, and a shadow covered us.

"Watch out," said Tony, pulling us closer to the cliff face.

A large, muscular, cat-like creature, with thirty foot wings, four talons and a wiry mane around his head landed on the ground in front of us, eyeing us beadily from two golden orbs that shone above its aquiline beak.

"Ey!" said Tony, slapping the beast on its back in a disturbingly familiar way. "Griffone! Walter Burleigh, Griffone!"

"Hello, Tony," said the griffin, tossing his mane.

"Meet my friends, Harry, and Hannah. They got a message for you, Walter Burleigh, from the chairman."

"Come up to my eyrie," said Walter Burleigh. "Tony is my friend, and I am honoured to show hospitality to the friend of my friend. Come! I can take the two of you. Tony, I will come back for you."

He seemed to be offering his rear leg for us as a sort of step, so Hannah and I climbed onto his back.

Walter Burleigh flapped his wings and launched himself into the air, wrenching us upwards and forwards. I clinged to his neck, and Hannah held tightly onto me. He coasted for a moment, gliding down slightly, then flapped his wings again and made his way upwards, not without apparent effort.

At the top of the cliff face he suddenly turned and flew straight towards a rock pillar jutting outwards. Suddenly he veered downwards and to the left, sharp rocks whistled past our ears, and we found ourselves in a dark cave, with our eyes adjusting to the dim light.

He slid across the rocks, stopped still and nodded. We took it to mean that he wanted us to get off, so we did.

Walter Burleigh flew back out to get Tony.

Hannah and I looked around as our eyes adjusted to the darkness. It wasn't nearly as dark as I had thought.

The cave had clearly been hollowed out, for it was quite rectangular in shape, with straight and regular walls. Pots and plates were hanging from the wall just above a large fireplace in the centre, over which a large pot of stew was simmering. There was a bookshelf at the rear of the cave with a strange alphabet on the spines of the books that I had never seen before, and next to that ten or twelve cylindrical pots, taller than a man's height. There was also a skylight in the rear of the cave, through which the afternoon sun was still shining. The stained glass on the skylight bore a picture of a griffin next a boy, or perhaps it was a young elf, holding a sword.

The ground of the cave and the walls were covered with tiles painted with ornate, stylised pictures of griffins and what I took to be Tony's elves, gnomes and giants, together with more of the unusual writing. It looked like a cross between Chinese characters and the claw-scratchings of a chicken. Some of the characters were beautifully illuminated, in a medieval style, somewhat like I imagine the illuminations of the famous book of Kells to have been.

Walter Burleigh returned, and Tony leapt off his back.

"Welcome, son of Adam and daughter of Eve," said Walter Burleigh. "Welcome to my eyrie. I, Walter Burleigh, am your servant tonight. My griffin mate is out hunting, so I apologise that she cannot greet you as well at this time. My home is your home. My hearth is your hearth. My hospitality is yours, as custom demands."

And Walter Burleigh glided to the rear of his cave and began rummaging around in the large pots that were standing there.

Presently he returned with some herbs and spices and threw them in the stew.

Just then his griffin mate returned, flapping noisily through the cave mouth and screeching to a stop on the tiles. With a loud thump she threw down two dead goats, and then turned around and fixed me with her gaze.

"Two more humans. Friends of Tony's?"

"Yes," said Walter Burleigh, "Friends of Tony's."

"Welcome, friends of Tony. I am Mary Burleigh, griffin, and your servant. My home is yours, my hearth is yours."

I felt that something ought to be said in reply to such politeness, so I said, "Thank you, Mary and Tony. I am Harry - and this is Hannah - and we accept your offer of hospitality gratefully. Thank you very much."

Mary and Walter looked at each other.

I said, "Did I say something wrong?"

"Not at all," said Walter. "It's just that - you are very polite. Not many of the humans that we have met are polite."

Tony looked a little put out at this comment, so I tried to smooth things over.

"Oh, it's just that I'm a poet, I suppose. I like to put things poetically. I'm not that special, really - plenty of men and women are just as polite as we are."

"Say," said Tony, "You do look familiar, actually. Haven't I seen your face before? Are you some famous fellow, aren't you?"

"Henry Lawson, at your service. Harry is just what everybody calls me."

Without warning, Walter Burleigh put his beak near my hair and sniffed me.

"You and Hannah smell different from most humans, you know." And Hannah and I held our breaths, wondering if he could tell that we weren't really humans. "I'm not sure what it is. Something like mead, but stronger." I relaxed - he had simply smelled the alcohol fumes on me. Walter continued, "But it doesn't matter - excuse my rudeness. Come," he said, rolling out a barrel. "Join us in drinking the honey-nectar of the Mihalati."

"Mead," said Tony, licking his lips. "Honey beer, it is. The closest

60

thing to wine under the seven moons, and it goes down smooth-a, Mister Lawson, it does indeed. Makes one-a go all warm inside."

With one talon Walter took a mug from the wall, and with the other talon lifted up the barrel and poured a thick, golden liquid into the mug. He handed it to me but Hannah said, "No, Harry, you know you can't."

I protested, "But..."

"No," said Hannah firmly. "Or else, separate tents tonight."

I seriously considered drinking it, but Walter pulled back the mug before I could grab it.

"He's a drunkard, is he, Hannah?" asked Walter, shaking his head. "That's what that smell was! Some sort of disgusting earthly mead. Some griffins have the same problem. They end up flying in circles and swooping randomly and crashing, like jarabaleri - um - budgerigars - that have eaten too much fermented fruit, or they pick a fight with another griffin for a slight, stupid reason that no one would normally care about. There is no help for the disease of drunkenness, you know, Hannah, other than complete abstinence. Come, we will not drink mead at all tonight, Mister Lawson, in case it tempts you too much and you end up falling off the wagon, to use an Australyan expression that I have heard Tony use."

I was disappointed, but Hannah seemed pleased, so I let it pass.

After we had eaten, Walter Burleigh's expression turned serious. The sun had gone down, for there was no longer anything apart from faint moonlight shining through the skylight, and the red fireglow cast eerie flickers against the cave wall.

"It is the custom for us to tell tales, sagas and songs to one another after the evening meal. Come, Harry - first I shall tell my stories - then you and Hannah shall tell me yours.

"This world, our home-world, the realm of the seven moons, was once the home of the Evern Elves. But in the fourteenth age of your world, when the Roman Legions ruled on earth and the darkness was deepest, Heru, the king of the vine and the grain, was born as a human, Herushva. After Herushva died, slaughtered by the people of your world, the unfallen left the nine physical realms and went to dwell with him in the unworldly realms, the halls of the unknown god, which is where Herushva flew after Heru gave him wings.

"And in a vision given to Redrani the griffin, Heru led the clan of the griffins to this realm. And Redrani gave us a message. This is the message he told us.

"'Heruriannin said: You have have suffered the loss of your own world, for the Nomin have destroyed it. It has broken my heart to hear your cries, so I have heard you and answered you. Take the Evern world to be your own. It is your garden, to rule over and to cherish. Be good, wise rulers and I will bless the goats and sheep and make them multiply, and I will bless the berries and herb-roots and make them plentiful, and there will always be enough rain and enough sunshine.'

"So we came here, and we still dwell here today. This is the saga of Heru and the coming of the griffins to the Evern Realm."

Walter Burleigh adjusted his wings, and moved into a slightly more comfortable position by the fire.

"And now I shall tell you another story. The story of how I came to be called Walter Burleigh. Now, you see, several years ago I was seeking to construct a new eyrie, here, closer to the ley lines and the gate to the other worlds. Now it so happened that some griffins went to New York - in the Northern Union States of United America - and they asked the humans there if there were any other griffins in New York. They said there were no griffins but there was a man named Griffin - Walter Burleigh Griffin. They got to be friends with him, and he came through with them and they introduced him to me. That gateway emerged less than five miles from here - for some reason it was further south than yours. He was an architect - as I am also - but he had some new ideas, new building techniques, that they are using in a place called New York now, in the N.U.S.U.A.

"He taught me some of those techniques and we used them on this building - the use of reinforced concrete - structural supports of a type I had not seen before - we used these techniques to build this eyrie that you are in right now. Originally it was a much smaller cave, and the roof was quite unstable. Walter Burleigh showed me how to put reinforced concrete in the roof. The tiles come from New York, but the painting on the tiles was done by a local griffin.

"Now it so happened that one day a rogue troll infected with rabies came out of the forest attacked me while I was waiting for Walter Burleigh to arrive from New York. Walter Burleigh leapt out of the Aetheric gate and, seeing what has happening, immediately put himself between the troll and me - he took out a gun and shot it - but the troll leapt forward and bit him on the arm before it died.

"Walter Burleigh died slowly and agonisingly of rabies instead of me. It ought to have been me! - I had not seen the troll - had Walter Burleigh not come between me and the troll, I am certain it would have killed me. You see, I owe a human being my life.

"To keep his memory alive, in his honour, I, Emperor of the World of the Seven Moons, have forsaken my own name and taken his, and my griffin mate has taken his surname and a human name in his honour as well.

"And that is why I am called Walter Burleigh."

For a moment we were all silent, then Walter Burleigh leaned his beak towards me and said,

"Tony tells me you have a message from the chairman. Tell me this message - it can be your story. Your contribution to the sagas and tales tonight."

I swallowed nervously and leant over to speak to him.

"Well, Walter. Ah... Um... I must tell you that... our message is not exactly from the chairman. You might not be completely happy about this - um... but, Walter, I'm actually with the... Well, I'm on the side of the Robots, you see. And, knowing that you have made a treaty with the Marxians, I've come to put the other side of the story before you. Um. Your majesty. I feel that these are things you ought to know about. That's all."

I couldn't be sure what griffin facial expressions meant, but it seemed almost certain to me that Walter was looking distinctly angry. His brow was knitted, and his eyes had turned fiery.

And he wasn't the only one.

Tony, suddenly red-faced and shaking, blurted out, "But Harry - you tell me! You swear to me! You say to me-a you bring a message from-a the Chairman!"

"I'm sorry Tony - you have to understand - this is something Walter really needs to know! Everything in F.R.E.A.K.I.N. Australya is not what it seems. Things are rotten there, rotten to the core, Tony."

Tony spluttered and he brought his right fist down into the left one, with the gesture of an angry man hitting a table.

"What do you mean, Harry? If Harry's with the Robots, Walter, you can't trust one word he say! I am part of that... um... research, you know - the spying on Robots research - I knew they are planning this-a revolution-a. You must not trust Harry, Walter! Don't-a trust-a Harry, whatever you -"

Walter's eyes seemed to have turned completely red - he suddenly looked like a very devil from hell - he swivelled his head and stared at him so piercingly that I was suddenly very, very, very glad that I wasn't standing in Tony's boots.

"Thank you, Tony," said Walter coldly, "But I will make my own decisions as to whom to trust and not to trust. After all, I am the King. Go on, Harry."

I swallowed again. I had to come up with a fact, something that Walter Burleigh could verify. Something that would show him that he could trust me.

Walter looked at me intensely.

"Well, Harry?"

I cleared my throat.

"You can't trust the Marxians, Walter. They have been experimenting on griffins. Why, in the last year or two the government scientists took twenty three griffins around Kalgoorlie, not far from Okonna, where they had leaped through into our realm, looking for gold, apparently. And somehow the scientists got five griffin eggs as well - I don't know how. Overall they took thirty four gryphons and twelve eggs."

Hannah said, "Tell him what they did with them."

"They dissected the griffins and used their brains to construct the Aetheric Tunnel."

Suddenly Tony seemed to have gone very quiet, as though he was trying to shrink into the shadows.

"But that's ridiculous - we have not lost twenty three griffins in the last year," said Walter Burleigh. "Yes, we have had griffins go missing on unauthorised incursions to gather gold - I really don't know how you know that - over a long period, perhaps more than ten or fifteen - but in the past year or two we would have lost no more than three griffins, I believe. Certainly not twenty three." He snorted.

"See?" said Tony pointedly. "See? He's a liar. Blanky liar, Harry, that's-a what you are."

"It certainly appears that way," said Walter, eyeing us both suspiciously. "It certainly appears that way."

"I've come to plead with you, Walter," I said, feeling panic in my stomach, a kind of rising uneasiness. I wasn't thinking rationally at all. I began to beg. "Please don't help them - don't help the Marxians! Please - don't send your griffin army to help them, Walter, please. The Marxian government doesn't deserve it. They experimented on griffins - and humans - and they made the Robots out of dead people - even killed people - and babies - to make them. They are bad people, very bad people, Walter, please don't help them."

"I'm sorry, Harry," said Walter, "But I find your stories incredible, unbelievable. Clearly, if you are with the Robots, you are making these things up in order to try to convince me not to help them. It only convinces me further that the Robots ought to be opposed - these are unnatural creatures, things made of metal and animated by some sort of unholy necromancy, I wouldn't mind betting. And frankly, Harry, you smell wrong. I mean, you literally smell wrong. You stink of cogs and gears and circuits and switches - at first I thought that you might be one of the scientists, or that you stayed around Robots too long, but I don't think that's it. No, I wouldn't mind betting that you yourself are one of these mechanical men. I wouldn't mind betting you are some sort of mechanical contrivance meant to infiltrate communities of humans - I mean, a spy - a Robot spy, that they sent in to fool humans. Furthermore, I have my own honour to think of. I have made an agreement with the Marxians, to help them, in case the Robot rebellion should happen - and griffins are a people who keep their word! We are the honourable Nashar! If we are nothing else, we are honest, truthful, and if we make a promise it is never, ever broken, except under the most extreme circumstances. I would only break this promise if I was certain that the Marxians had been lying to me. And you have just convinced me otherwise."

"Um... Walter," said Mary, who was cleaning the pots and pans. "Um - can you help me over here? I mean really, it is a bit inconsiderate to make me do it all myself."

Walter ignored her, for his speech was now in full flow, "And now, Harry, listen to this! It appears that you have brought me that very news - that the Robot rebellion has indeed happened - the very news that tells me the time for keeping my promise is here! There is much to be done. We must assemble the griffin flotilla - the army of the skies. We must prepare the griffin army for the journey across the branches of the World-Tree."

"Walter," said Mary. "The washing up? Come and help me!" Strangely, her interjection made me think I had forgotten to mention something to Walter, but I couldn't think what it might be.

"Walter," said Mary, "There's something I need to ask - a nagging thought. I was just wondering if -"

Walter ignored her. He leapt up in the segreant pose, wings open, talons bared against an imaginary enemy and delivered a ringing chant.

"The time has come for the griffins to cast their wings across the Aether, for the raptors to dance on the winds of the worlds, in the greatest cause of all! Friendship! The Marxians call on us, and we must answer!" He lifted a clenched talon towards the heavens.

"Walter," Mary said again. "I have something to-"

"Not now, Mary," interrupted Walter, the flow of his speech completely lost. He shook his mane and gave her a look that was full of condescension.

"Griffin mate, I must deliver these humans back to the forest floor. We cannot keep them under the protection of my wings - and our cave roof - as our guests any more. They came into my eyrie under false pretenses - they lied to us! - in the sight of griffins this is the most grievous sin any Nasharae can commit. These humans are no more our friends than any Nomina was ever a friend of Avadorin and the boy, they are no less our enemies than Heru himself and Pazor are enemies. No, they must be returned to the world they came from. Etmekva alva todad matim disa. Truth is as truth does."

He turned to look at us, with the knee of his rear talon bent toward us, he clearly intended for us to get up onto his back. Hannah was trembling now.

I said, "Hannah, it will be fine."

I lifted her up and put her on first.

Then I got up behind her.

The griffin lifted off, and swooped downwards dangerously fast.

Upon reaching the ground, we leapt off quickly, and Walter suddenly turned segreant, talons upwards, wings open, facing us, and said, "Get away! Off with you! Into the bush! If I ever see you again in this forest I will treat you as you deserve! Look at my talons," he said, flexing his foretalons at us. He slashed a tree, making bark and splinters of wood fly off and leaving a great gash in it, that a chainsaw would not have been able to make so quickly. "My talons! How they slash! Look at how strongly my beak grips! You will be treated like enemies if you come into my sight, or if I even catch even a whiff of you, ever again."

Hannah was standing completely still, she was clearly in shock. I shoved her out into the forest, and she came to herself and started running, stumbling over branches and whimpering, and I followed her, running as fast as I could. As we ran I could still hear Walter's voice echoing amongst the trees, saying, "Mark my words! You will be mince-meat if I ever so much as catch a whiff of you, Harry and Hannah! Mark my words! Mince-meat!"

And we ran for quite some time, until we could no longer hear his voice at all. It must have been a good hour and a half later when we stopped running because neither of us could run any more.

We slumped down onto a log. I took out some matches and gathered the dryest sticks I could find and we built a small fire, and I took the water from our canteens and made us both a cup of billy tea. As we drank I tried to keep the fire burning well, so that it didn't make much smoke.

After we had finished the cup of tea and Hannah had calmed down a little, I said, "Well, I think that qualifies as an answer. We can go home now and tell them that the king of the griffins said no." Hannah laughed then, and I felt a little better about it all.

But then Hannah said, "I think I'll check the chronometer - find out how long it is until we can go home."

She rummaged in her swag.

"Do you know, I don't think I can find it."

She took everything out and laid it out on the ground, the tent, the salted meat, the tea, the billy, knives and forks and spare jumper and everything else, and then rummaged in the swag again.

She turned the swag inside it. It was very clear that the chronometer was not in it.

"It's not here, Harry. Maybe it's in your swag."

"I'm certain I didn't take it off you. There's no way I can imagine it ending up in my swag, but I'll look anyway."

I took my swag and looked through it, then did the same thing, laying out the contents on the forest floor.

There was no sign of the Chronometer in my luggage either.

Tears filled Hannah's eyes. "We're stuck here, Harry," she said, "I've lost the Chronometer. Where could it be? I packed it so carefully, it couldn't have fallen out."

Then we looked at each other.

"Tony!" we both said in unison, and I felt my ire rising.

Hannah looked again at our possessions. "Do you know what else is missing, Harry. The blanky guns. The guns are gone."

"That blanky thief," I said, stamping around the campfire. "That bally, blankity, blanking blankity-blank." (Of course, those are not the real words I used, but the real words are not decent to print in a book.)

"Harry," said Hannah, "Foul language is not helping things!"

"Sorry, Hannah," I said, and sat down next to her and tended to the fire. "We've got to keep the fire from smoking too much, or else that bally griffin will be after us."

Hannah started weeping. She sobbed out, "What are we going to do?"

I moved next to her and held her close to me and said, "Even if we're stuck here, Hannah, at least we have each other. At least I have you, my spirit girl - in the flesh." I chuckled. "Or should I say, in the cogs and gears and oil and lubricating fluids - everything that I love, Hannah, everything that is you. I really love you, you know."

And then I looked at her, wiped away a tear from her cheek, and she smiled back at me through tear-filled eyes.

"Tears," she said, "Harry, the scientists even gave us tears."

And then an interesting thought came to me.

I said, "Of course, all we really need to do is find Tony..."

CHAPTER 14: TRICKSTER

Strangely enough, all these troubles brought us closer together. The love between us was more consolation than you can imagine, in the shadow of that dark, griffin-haunted forest.

Her kisses, the touch of her soft hands. Our fingers intertwining in passion.

And the way her fingers danced across a scar on my elbow as we sat together by the campfire afterwards - it was a scar from when I fell from that cliff, years ago - a scar that may or may not be real.

Hannah accepted everything about me - that was what that night meant to me.

And I remember reflecting to myself sadly that the troubles I shared with Bertha never brought Bertha and I closer together. Though of course, I didn't really know how many of my memories of Bertha were real, and how many were transplanted from the real Harry.

It's typical isn't it - every good memory we have is intertwined with regrets and sadness. Every good experience in our lives seems so partial, so very incomplete.

I wondered if that was the incompleteness of being a Robot, of not being fully human?

Or do humans experience life that way too?

We both slept well that night, once we finally decided to go to sleep.

In the morning, as we packed up the campsite quietly and efficiently, I realised that the simple fact of Hannah's presence brought me a great deal of comfort. We were a team, as closely knit as any shearing team or group of mates working together that I, or Harry before me, had ever known.

I resolved never to drink again. I was not ever going to ruin this happiness.

But I knew I probably would drink. I'm a drunkard. There's some things you can't change.

Once we were packed up, we held each other closely for a moment.

It's amazing how precious human touch is - when you've been on your own, alone, like I had in that prison cell, deprived of human contact - a simple hug like that is more wonderful than you can imagine.

Then Hannah said, "So what now, Harry?"

"I suppose we'll have to head back. Well, I mean, either we try to find the mesa again, or go back to the griffin's eyrie and find Tony, wherever he is."

Hannah thought for a moment.

"Well, Harry, I think it might be easier to find the mesa if we start from the griffin's eyrie. And that has the advantage of being the same place Tony is starting from."

How competent Hannah is - I thought to myself - such an intelligent person. And much braver than me.

"Alright," I said, trying not to let my voice tremble. "To the eyrie it is."

And we set off.

It took us a good two Ours of walking briskly before we found ourselves coming towards the base of the mountain. It was a heavily vegetated part of the forest with lots of tree cover and fairly thick scrub, mostly bracken and other ferns. We could see the cliff face far above us, so we knew where we were headed.

But then we heard it - a sound somewhat like an eagle's cry.

An indistinct shadow went over us.

I pulled Hannah into the darkest place I could find, underneath a large deciduous tree with enormous, twisting branches, and whispered, "It's Walter. It's sure to be Walter."

As if in answer, Walter's voice echoed from above, growling, crying out, "Hannah! Harry! Where are you! Come out, wherever you are!"

Hannah froze. She whispered through clenched teeth, "He knows we're here. He's trying to get us to come out, so he can kill us! He wants to slash us with those talons!"

We heard Walter's voice again, coming closer, crying out, "Halloa! I don't want to hurt you! It's alright! You can come out, little humans!

Come out! Don't worry, I won't hurt you!" We could hear his wings flapping somewhere above us.

"That trickster!" I whispered. "What a liar. And a hypocrite. It was our supposed lies that he was so upset about."

Hannah said, "He's trying to convince us that everything is alright! Then he'll turn on us and say, 'Didn't I tell you not to come around here?' then, SLASH, and we will be dead, Harry, dead."

"I know you're out here somewhere," cried Walter. "Somewhere - and Tony has your chronometer - so you have probably come back to get it. Come out! Come out, wherever you are! Don't be afraid. I'm here to help you!"

This abominable charade continued for at least an hour, with Hannah and I trembling in the shadows. If I had had a gun or rifle with me I would most certainly have shot the griffin as he passed overhead, but I had nothing, not even a slingshot with a pebble in it.

Finally the griffin seemed to tire of his efforts, and he disappeared aloft.

We made our way up the mountain. When we got to the base of the cliff, we found the nearest accessible hiding place, which turned out to be an enormous fig tree. We hid among the branches, behind the large leaves, and watched and waited for Tony to show up.

"He could have gone already," I said. "The fact that Walter knows Tony has the chronometer indicates that Tony has been to the eyrie recently. But if Tony doesn't turn up in the next half-Our or so, I suppose we'll set off in the direction of the mesa."

It was coming close to mid-morning now. If we set a good pace we might make it back to the mesa before dark. If we could find it, that is.

Hannah seemed to read my thoughts.

"Providing the sun's direction here is fairly constant - and I think it is; it looked as though it rose in the same place this morning as yesterday, between the mountains - then we should be able to make it back to the mesa, Harry. We'll just follow the river, then that little stream, then continue with the sun behind us."

The sun moved up across the sky and we waited, with no sign of the griffin or Tony. After another long period of waiting silently, Hannah said, "Harry, I think we should set off. Perhaps Tony has already gone."

So we starting walking back down. We reached the base of the mountain quickly, and had been going through dense forest for a short while when something rustled above us.

I looked up. Through a small gap in the leaves I caught a glimpse of griffin feathers, and heard the sound of large wings flapping. I grabbed Hannah again and pulled her close to me and we stayed still, for quite a while, simply waiting.

It was nice holding her close.

"I can't believe he's still looking for us," I whispered.

Soon, he was gone again, and we were on our way. We followed the river for a long while, and stopped for lunch in a grassy knoll near a large blueberry bush, not long after we reached the tributary.

As we ate the last of our supplies, Hannah took my hand in hers and said, "Harry. There's something I've been meaning to tell you. A confession really, that I ought to make, ah, something that... I should have told you before."

She was looking at me terribly earnestly, with those brown eyes of hers.

I said, "What? What is it, Hannah?"

"Harry... I had two jobs when I was working at the Robot factory. I wasn't just an engineer - the government had another job for me - I was assigned, part-time, to perform surveillance on... certain individuals... people of interest to the authorities."

"But... what does that have to do with chemical engineering?"

"Actually, I did a double major in chemical engineering and manufacturing Robotics. Well, actually, perhaps it was the real Bertha. I'm really not sure if I did it or if it was her... I don't know when I was made, where her memories end and mine begin. But you see, I was assigned to watch the new Robots - the ones that thought they were human, Harry. You were one of them. The main one. They made me watch you; I saw the troubles you had with Bertha. Your drunken episodes, the sorry life you were living... Harry, I'm sorry. It was a betrayal, but I didn't have any choice."

I was so stunned by this news that I couldn't talk.

"There were others, Harry, even some of the party functionaries, ones that had been taken away to the camps, to be replaced with Robots... That job was what turned me into an insurgent, Harry. Seeing the lies, the terrible things they were doing..."

"You watched me? So they had cameras in the house? I knew it..."

"That was when I fell in love with you, Harry. I watched you through cameras that were in your walls, listened to the bugs that were recording you and Bertha, and watched you through the eyes of your Robot, when you were at home, before you went to Marx Zealand. I'm so sorry, Harry... And when you were in Marx Zealand as well, I was the one assigned to watch you... Until the day you sabotaged your Robot's surveillance circuits, and the bugs in your house... I was in love with you by then - do you know, I protected you. I didn't tell them that you had destroyed the microphones - I simply told them that someone spilled water on them. And there was a camera - I managed to disable it - by sabotaging the receiver."

"Why did they want you to watch me?"

"One of my main tasks was to see if you realised you were a Robot... It was terribly moving, seeing you watching your Robot - seeing you realise that he had a human soul - that he was human, in a way - when perhaps it was the fact that you were seeing yourself in him..."

"So, when I came to the factory, were you assigned to contact me then?"

"No, that was completely from me... I was part of the Resistance by then... They needed me more in the factory - anyone could do the surveillance, but my specialised scientific skills were needed there at that time... The day I saw you walking around in the factory I couldn't believe my eyes - I felt as though I knew you intimately. I mean, I really did."

"It's very strange," I said. "I don't know what to think about it. Perhaps that's why I felt as though I already knew you."

"I already loved you, Harry. From the first day I was given the assignment, from the very first day I watched you through those cameras. And after I finished at the Surveillance Unit I went and found all your old books on the black market and read them. I know your poetry, your poems. Faces in the Street, Freedom on the Wallaby. And your stories... The Loaded Dog... The Drover's Wife..."

"Those poems weren't mine, Hannah... They were the real Henry Lawson's poems."

"True enough... But I am sure that the real Hannah and the real Henry Lawson would have fallen in love, had they met, in some other world, just as we did... Just as the Robot versions did... Some things are meant to be, Harry..."

Strangely enough, I felt a guilty pang at that.

I had been unfaithful to Bertha - even though, really, I hadn't been married to her, but I had believed that I was married to her. It was so complex, and I hardly knew what was true.

I had such mixed feelings about it all.

I wasn't sure how to feel about Hannah watching me. It was strange and creepy - but this was the world we were living in under the Marxians. Everyone watching each other. Perhaps Bertha was reporting on me too. It wasn't unknown.

"I wonder if Bertha..."

"You're free now, Harry. You were never really married to Bertha. You're free to love me."

She reached forward and embraced me, kissed me slowly, but a thought struck me. I stopped kissing her and asked, "What if... What if Bertha was a Robot, too?"

"No, she wasn't. She was the original. I was assigned to watch her - to see if she noticed any differences. She didn't."

"She didn't even know I was a cuckoo in the nest..."

We kissed.

It was strange - For some reason I suddenly felt more myself, than I ever had. At last I seemed to know who I was at last.

The kiss lingered.

I glanced over Hannah's shoulder.

There were dark funeral clouds over most of the sky behind her, but the sun was shining through a gap in the clouds, and the light shone on the tops of the trees, making this strange world look like a fairy-tale forest.

She was the princess of a fairy-tale world.

And as we kissed I remembered a phrase I had read somewhere, "The truth will set you free."

Then two dark moons were drifting by the edges of the gap in the clouds, slowly, uncertain whether they ought to try to eclipse the sun, for both were too small.

I realised Hannah and I were at the centre of events that promised to change Australya. Would we ever get back there? And would anything we did really change a thing?

And why should I care about whether we could change anything? Did it really matter?

And why did such thoughts intrude in moments that should the happiest moments of my life? Here I was, kissing Hannah and thinking such thoughts. Was it some sort of disorder in the instructions they put in my Babbage Comptroller Brain? A mistake the scientists had made when they made me?

Did humans, or other Robots suffer such thoughts? I doubted it.

And then her mouth was so soft and her embrace was so gentle, so comforting, so complete, that it seemed to me as though no pain or grief could ever touch me again. I knew in that moment that I loved her with every inch of my being, every cog and gear of my body, every circuit and wire of my electric brain and every brace, buttress and bolt of my metal skeleton. I loved her completely, and would love her forever.

That one single embrace can do accomplish so much, make you certain of something that was a mere possibility beforehand, is a sort of a miracle, really...

Suddenly the hole in the clouds got larger and the sun shone brighter; the beauty of the scene behind Hannah's shoulder seemed like a halo surrounding her head, as though heaven confirmed everything I felt. Then a gentle rain began to plop down, with the sun behind it shining through and making the raindrops look like diamonds glittering down - a sunshower - with the grey of the clouds behind it. So beautiful.

It suited Hannah's gentleness, the gentleness of her touch, the softness in the way she kissed me, so well.

Gentle, warm raindrops fell on us, like tears of gladness.

Perhaps we could stay here. This world - beautiful, untouched, the perfection of wildness - a world of giant forests, tall trees, high mountains, and impassible cliffs... and dangerous griffins and who-knows-what-else...

And suddenly there was two men standing there, wearing the uniforms of high-ranking security officers. One was short and balding, the other, tall with brown hair and a Roman nose. They were both holding revolvers pointed at us.

The shorter man said, "Henry Lawson and Hannah Thornburn, we are arresting you for treason and conspiracy against the Marxian State. Stand up and put your hands up."

We did as he said. The tall man waved his gun at us.

"Walk ahead of us. We are heading towards the location of the Aetheric Gateway. You will come through with us, and your trial for treason will take place back in Australya, in the Army Research faciity in Sydney."

We walked through the forest for half an hour, and they said very little. Eventually we saw the faint blue light of an Aetheric Gateway ahead of us.

"Quick," said the short man. "We're not too late for this one."

"Hurry!" said the tall one. "The next portal won't open for at least five weeks. It's a shame we can't use the Kanberra one - it's much more powerful."

We started running. But just as we reached the clearing the Aetheric

Gateway winked shut, and the two men cursed.

"Blankity blank. We'll have to tie you up," said the short man. He pulled out several pieces of rope from his backsack and began to do just that, starting with me.

A gunshot sounded, then another.

The two men keeled over, red patches appearing on their shirts over the heart.

Tony walked out from among the trees, pointing one of the pistols he had stolen from our swags directly at me.

The strange thought came to me that even here, in a world ruled by sharp-taloned griffins, the most dangerous animal was man.

Chapter 15: Where, When and How

Keeping the gun trained on my forehead, Tony took out the chronometer and waved it in front of my face.

"They are not going to be the heroes that arrest Harry and Hannah. I am. And I get to go home. You not tell me about your chronometer, Hannah, Harry, how it-a-worka. When I come through here years ago, I have a different one, it not worka the same way as the new ones. And you forget to tell me how many Ours."

I frowned.

"That's our chronometer, Tony. It belongs to us."

He wagged his finger at me.

"Ah, not any more, Harry. Tut-tut, you don't thinka that way. I'm in charge now, and that make-a me in the right. But let me tell you how this is-a-going to be. You will tell me how many days til the doorway appear again. Or I will shoot-a Hannah."

He moved the gun so that it was pointing at Hannah's head now.

My resistance simply crumbled.

"Alright, it's thirty six Ours."

Tony said, "Ah, good, then your gateway, it's a much less time than this one. We must get to your gateway, then. Hurry. Get walking. I want to go home and have a bath. And a beer."

"Well done, Harry," said Hannah crossly, "You've taken away our bargaining power." I winced.

Tony shoved the gun in my side. "Stop talking. Harry and Hannah, you need to show me where the doorway is going to appear - take me there. And then we will wait until the doorway appears."

And so we trudged back through the forest, with Tony holding the gun on us, trying to find our way back to the small stream we had been following when we had encountered the security agents. The clouds gathered above us and it began raining, and the ground became muddy, every second step seemed to be through a muddy puddle, and then the rain began to fall harder and I began to think that we might escape.

But Tony grabbed Hannah's arm and pushed the gun into her side. I knew nothing about Robot anatomy, but judging from how vulnerable we both were in so many ways, I didn't have any confidence that the scientists had made us immune to gunshots, any more than any human was.

The walk seemed to take longer than it should have. Finally the rain stopped, and we kept trudging onwards through mudpatches and puddles. The Ours lagged and we finally found ourselves walking towards the mesa as the sun was setting.

Then we were standing on the mesa, waiting for the doorway to appear. Tony looked at the chronometer. "Read it," he said to Hannah - he had already worked out that I wasn't good at technical things - and she said, "There's five Ours to go before the gateway appears."

I felt disturbed by this. I whispered, "I thought time was going much slower here."

"It's been accelerating," she whispered back.

"What are you a-saying?" demanded Tony.

Hannah said loudly, "Time - Harry thought it goes slower here - but it's been accelerating. I suspect that the four dimensions of each world are orbiting one another - it's some sort of exponential thing. Five Ours is my best guess."

The gun Tony was holding clicked as he cocked the firing lever.

"Well, too bad about being a hero. It looks as though I have to waste you two. Can't have you going back and telling the Robots about me, stealing your chronometer, and that I was an agent for the government, can I? I went through a funny blue thing, and find myself there in the parliament, that's all. And I'm on their side. I support-a the Robot struggle. Ha! That's what I will say."

Hannah asked, "How did you know about the parliament?"

"I was watching you, listening to a-you. You are lucky the griffin didn't get you first. I will make it a quick end. That a-griffin - he woulda make it a slow, painful end. You ever see a griffin talons open up the side of a reindeer bull? Now, you first - one, two..."

Trying to get extra time, I said, "Wait! Please give Hannah and me a chance to say goodbye, Tony. Please. Show a bit of compassion. And I need my last smoke."

"No - it might be too hard for me to do it if I think-a of you as human beings. You meana nothing to me. An it's stupid - I don't a believe in this talking a lot-a-about what you are doing - like a villain in some sorta melodrama film. No chit chat. No talk. No gloating. No, I just do. Not like those-a stupida movie where he talk-a talk-a, give the people a chance to think of how to get out of it. It's just stupida. I not do that - not chit-chat - no blah, blah, blah..."

I snapped.

"Oh, for God's sake, Tony, just get on with it. As if isn't bad enough that you're killing us, but you've got to bore us half to death first with this bally claptrap."

With a hostile growl from the back of his throat, Tony cocked the gun again, and I said to myself, you've done it now, Harry. We're done for, and it's all my fault.

Suddenly the air beside Tony shimmered. A tiny pinpoint of blue aetheric light appeared, floating about three feet above the ground.

Stepping backwards in surprise, Tony said, "Five Ours? Looks like it's a starting already. It should be up and running in an Our or two, then..."

He turned to face us, with the gun still pointed at my head. He placed the barrel of the gun squarely between my eyes. Well this is it Harry - no getting away from this one. Looks like its curtains for Henry Lawson number two.

Tony said, "Well, I got to do it now. No more delays. Don't want to risk-a that they come through and find you here. I shoot you then throw the bodies over the cliff-a. I do-a you first, Harry. One...."

Behind Tony's shoulder the light expanded, slowly at first, then more quickly, swirling strangely.

"Two..."

Then, very suddenly, the blue light exploded into a full sized Aetheric entry portal. Even as Tony said, "Three," four Robots leaped through into existence in this world.

I saw it happening. I don't know if everything was going slowly, like they say it does when your life is at risk, or if the scientists had designed me so that my Robot senses come into play at those extreme moments. But in the very last moment before Tony's index finger depressed the trigger, I watched one Robot leap through the air between him and me, shielding me from the oncoming bullet. I saw another grab Tony's arm, disarming him in an instant, and I saw the third leap in front of Hannah to protect her, and the fourth had leaped up and grabbed the bullet out of the very air even as it left the pistol barrel.

"What in the blinkin' blankety blank," said Tony, finding himself lying on the ground, dazed, cradling his broken right arm, with a Robot sitting on him.

"We heard what was happening," said the Robot that was sitting on Tony. "We worked out how to use the Chronometer to communicate - there is a microphone in it, you see - we found the instruction booklet - it told us how to activate the Chronometer microphone remotely. But we hadn't worked out how to talk to you through it yet."

The Robot in front of me turned around and said, "Are you alright, Mister Lawson? No broken bones or gunshot wounds?"

"No, I'm fine. Completely alright."

"Well, hurry then, Harry." He seemed not to realise how comical the phrase sounded, which made me guffaw slightly. "Harry, we must go back. Events are already in motion. You must tell Toc what is happening - the government forces are beginning their final attack."

We hurried through the Aetheric Gateway and emerged into the basement room. The Robots at the console looked up at us as we came through.

The Robots brought Tony through as well. One of the Robots quickly found a medical kit, while the one that had brought him through took hold of his arm on both sides of the break, with one swift, powerful movement, reset the bone. Tony gave a loud scream of pain, and then whimpered as the Robot that had brought the medical kit through tied a splint onto it and made a sling.

Tony moaned, "What are you going to do with me?"

One of the Robots said, "Prevent you from doing any further harm."

Chapter 16: Back Home

Toc met us soon afterwards.

"Hello Harry. Hello Hannah. Good to see that you have both returned safe and uninjured. Things here have gotten worse since you left. The government forces are preparing for the final attack soon. We're getting our defenses ready, but I am afraid we won't be able to stand against them, particularly if Walter Burleigh arrives with the griffins, to support them."

He put his Robot hand on my shoulder and looked me in the eyes.

"I hope you have good news for us, Harry."

I shook my head - I felt guilty, as though Hannah and I hadn't tried hard enough - but there was very little else we could have done.

"I'm afraid I don't have good news, Toc. The griffin Walter Burleigh refused to believe anything I said. He simply would not accept that the Marxians had lied to him, and he told me that a griffin once he has given his word on something would never break it. I am afraid that an aerial army of griffins is still coming to help the Marxians - and Walter Burleigh didn't even believe me when I told him they were abducting griffins and experimenting on them."

Toc shook his head. "Our best calculations indicate that the Marxians are going to win, Harry. There is a small chance that we might hold our own, at least, if they don't get help from the griffins. But if the griffins come and fight for them, we're done for. Finished. We'll be decimated."

"What a terrible way to go," I wailed, suddenly feeling very dismal. After finding Hannah again, our lives were about to be cut short.

With a desperate glint in his eye, Toc said, "Harry, is there no way? Couldn't you go back and try again? Talk him around, convince him?"

"No," I said. "Walter Burleigh threatened to kill us if we came anywhere near his eyrie. There is simply no way he will ever agree to go back on his word. He was completely adamant."

Something in Toc's head whirred, as though his brain was putting in an extra effort to calculate a way for us out of the predicament we were in.

After standing stock-still for about twenty seconds, Toc said, "There is nothing for it but to put in our best effort. Perhaps something will change."

And suddenly he was a blur of activity. "We need reinforcements on the ground floor! The Robots with the best targeting programs, up to the second floor as snipers, and take the grenade launchers onto the roof! Activate all the defenses in the building itself - the Marxians had it well set up - get the windows covered - the ground floor doors need to be locked and bolted. I need someone to get down into the basement and fire up the old diesel generator as well! We may need extra power - the reactor tower is probably the first thing they will target. And we need to set aside an area for emergency repairs, maintenance and salvage - there will be many Robots injured today and some will be damaged beyond repair. There is no point wasting the cogs and circuits of defunct Robots when we may well need their parts for others."

And suddenly the whole place was buzzing like a beehive with Robots running here and there, carrying guns and rifles and grenade launchers to and fro, as well as tools and materials for strengthening the defenses.

The doors were fortified with extra steel and metal window shutters began covering all the windows. Large weapons, with a barrel the size of a large drainpipe - I don't know what they shot, but they were larger than any of the guns I had ever seen before - were moved up onto the roof. I can only imagine the government had them stored somewhere in Parliament House, thinking they would need them for their own defenses, never imagining that the Robots would be using their own weapons against them one day.

You can imagine how useless Hannah and I felt in the midst of all of that, and that feeling must have shown somehow, for one of the Robots came up to us, handed us two guns and said, "Come on, Mister Lawson, you and Miss Thornburn can help in our struggle." I felt relieved, and reflected that the Robots really showed much more human sensitivity than

I had expected. Then I remembered that I am a Robot, and wondered if I just thought they were sensitive because they could understand me.

We found places in the upper windows, where we could peer out through the barricades.

With the sound of guns firing the fighting began.

It brought back the days of the revolution to me. The confusion, the bloodshed, the way the sounds of fighting arrived from different directions, distant and near, the shouts and cries, indistinct mechanical noises, roaring engines and explosions.

Except this was really happening - the revolution was one of the real Harry's memories.

It was strange how little we knew of what was really happening. Hannah and I stayed at our post and shot at anything that we could glimpse through the smoke and confusion - part of a Marxoskeleton suit, or the turret of a tank, or a soldier aiming his rifle in our direction - but I doubt we hit anything. I've had a go at shooting a rifle in the bush - or, rather, the real Harry did, whose memories I share - but even when the target was a tin can that wasn't moving I was barely able to hit it.

Toc turned up after a little while. "I thought I would keep you informed about the progress of the battle, Harry and Hannah."

"But aren't you supposed to be commanding the Robot forces, Toc? Aren't you wasting time talking to us."

"Oh, goodness me, telling you what's happening won't take much concentration. With the radiophonic links we have established between us, Harry, I can do the commanding... um... internally. I do not need to talk out loud to command the forces. At the same time I can keep you informed."

His eyes took on a faraway aspect (it still seems a little strange saying that, but after I found out that I was a Robot I hadn't minded seeing them as expressive as people, in their own peculier mechanistic way) It seemed to me that Toc was looking deep within himself.

He intoned, "To the north is the main body of the besieging force, but we are surrounded on every side. At the moment our main effort is being put towards grappling with the new, more agile Marxoskeletons. . We have overcome the tanks, in the main - they are vulnerable to having their tread removed, and the main gun turret can be easily disabled by bending the barrel of the gun. The soldiers have been something a challenge because we don't want to hurt them - but conversely, most of them are carrying weapons that are little or no threat to us, such as rifles and pistols. Those carrying more dangerous weapons, Gatling guns and grenade launchers, have been dealt with already."

"Wait a moment - there's something new."

Bertha and I looked through our narrow little window, and saw something approaching from the northeast, that looked like ants swarming over the hill.

Toc twitched strangely, and said, "They are coming from the army base. Very swift - what are they? We've just lost twelve. Fifteen Robots. We've lost thirty. We're readjusting our tactics in response. Evasive manouevring. These things - they are small and very agile and they are very many - wait - one of them has been captured... They're bringing it in right now."

His eyes cleared and he looked straight at us. "Come! Down to the laboratory. We must find out what these things are."

We followed Toc downstairs at a breakbolt pace. We chased a small crowd of Robots carrying something into the laboratory.

It was made entirely of black metal, with nine or ten limbs spidering out from a cylindrical centre, and seven or eight cameratronic eyes around the cylinder in a seemingly random arrangement. The legs of the thing were still twitching slightly, despite the fact that the rear of the cylinder had been badly crushed.

The Robots placed the device on the examining table and attacked it with an inert gas scalpel. The cylinder quickly succumbed to the bright electrical point of the implement, breaking open like a clam shell to yield its secrets.

There was an incomprehensible mess of wires, circuits, relays, and what looked like miniature valves inside. Four Robots brought over microscopes and began examining it, and I certainly got the impression that they were communicating their findings to one another radiophonically.

They looked up.

One of the Robots said, "This thing is a travesty. It has a sophisticated Babbage Difference Engine - but no Aetheric Pattern! It is a calculating machine - an electronic brain with all the power of our Robot brains - but possessing no soul."

They all went silent and looked at one another.

Toc said, "These sorts of things were tried, once, but abandoned. They could not adapt themselves to human needs - humans found themselves adapting to the Babbage Comptroller Brain in such Robots - rather than the Robots adapting themselves to human interaction."

One of the other Robots said, "Humans seem unable to avoid travesties. This thing is as great a danger to them as it is to us - an automatic killing machine - with no soul - it cannot even distinguish between a man and a tree."

Toc agreed. "This is worse than a Robot servant. It could exterminate a child or a friend of the person who pressed the start button on it with no more compunction than a man stepping on an ant accidentally."

Suddenly someone started laughing - a loud, crass laughter that sounded out of place in there, among a crowd of Robots.

It was one of the members of the Supreme Council. For some reason he had been brought down to the laboratory - I wondered if the Robots had been examining him to see if he was human, or a Robot in human form like me - he was sitting there, tied to a chair, but he did not have a gag in his mouth, more's the pity.

"It makes me laugh!" he said, "You don't have a chance. We prepared these machines long ago - when we first made you - we made these machines to exterminate you - if you ever proved troublesome. The very same quality that makes you able to sympathise with humans - able to work with us - is the quality that makes you dangerous and unstable. The soul - is something we have tried to eliminate in the population at large! And here we were, putting souls in Robots. I told them, don't do it! Don't you see - you're just making the same mistake! Sooner or later you will have to put them down like rabid dogs! Well, they heeded my comments enough to make these things - machines that are programmed for one purpose only - to destroy Robots with Aetheric Patterns!"

One of the Robots pleaded with him, "But how can you say that when you, sir, are one of us? As I have been telling you, you have no flesh and blood - you are not human-bodied - you are entirely wire and cog - and in your head you have an electromatic brain with an Aetheric Pattern - circuits and wires - you are a Robot just like Mister Lawson and Miss Thornburn. And me. Don't you realise? Don't you understand? You are one of us!"

"Pah - I don't believe that at all. You're a liar." But he looked uncertain.

Toc, ignoring him, looked distant again and said, "These spider-things are turning the tide of the battle against us. We must prepare ourselves to be overcome. Come - we must go upstairs. We must seal ourselves in. We must close every window, every door, every space that one of these soulless spider-travesties can use to invade the parliament."

We went upstairs, where the Robots were already sealing off all the windows and doors.

One of the front doors suddenly opened, and a great crowd of Robots who had been outside rushed in in a mass, many of them struggling with the spider-contraptions, some with more than one attached to them, drilling holes in their carapaces, or attacking their eyes.

Bertha and I joined in the attempt to free the Robots from these things, and hundreds of Robots poured out from the stairwell, from the basement, carrying inert gas scalpels, welding equipment, flame throwers, and machine pistols - in short, anything with a fairly small range of influence that could be used against the spider-contraptions.

The doors slammed shut and were bolted behind the last Robot, and the battle with the spider-contraptions continued.

After a long, drawn out, deadly battle, ten more Robots were lying dead, but all of the spider-things that had come in with them through the door were lying on the floor, squashed, disabled, or destroyed.

Suddenly we heard a scuttling sound coming from outside, from every possible direction, and we could well imagine the spider-contraptions crawling over the whole building, looking for weaknesses, flaws in our workmanship, places to enter.

We could hear metal pincers scraping, scratching, bending and peeling, trying to lift the window covers up or pry them open or force a small gap to become a larger one.

It was completely terrifying.

Then as quickly as the terrific ordeal had begun, the sounds faded and our terror abated. I could almost imagine the spider-things scuttling back to their places behind the army ranks.

Then I heard a distant, muffled sound, as though someone was talking just outside.

At that moment another Robot strode forwards.

Toc acknowledged him and he began to speak.

"Master Toc - there is a man addressing us from the army ranks, on a Salpinxafone. He is advising us to surrender. He promises safe passage - he says if you come out onto the roof and talk to him there they will not set the arachnodrones on you - he says there is enough space that you will see them coming."

Toc immediately went up the stairway, and Hannah and I followed him.

We were standing at the top of the stairway, near the ladder that led to the manhole that went up onto the roof, when Toc turned around and said, "There is no need for you to risk your lives, Harry and Hannah. I am perfectly capable of carrying out these negotiations alone. I will be in contact with all the Robots, you know, via the abbreviated system of radiophonic telegraph we have access to internally."

I said, "Toc, I consider you a friend. I could hardly go out there and fight. But at least I can support you in this moment, in your ultimate hour of need. Heaven knows, this might be the end, and I just want to die knowing I've done at least one thing right in my life."

Toc said, "Harry, no. You don't have to do it. You've done enough - for goodness' sake - you went to the other World - you sought out their king, Walter Burleigh Griffin. You have already risked your life for us. For us all."

"Toc - no - you need me. I know how humans think - in many of the ways that count I am one of them. You need my advice at this juncture. You need my experiences - the real Henry Lawson's life experiences - to advise you. Humans are not trustworthy - for Marx's sake look at me. I go back to the drink at the drop of a hat. I'm completely unreliable. Bertha couldn't reliable on me at all. You need me out there with you, to tell you not to trust the humans, to remind you that they are all liars."

Suddenly another Robot appeared at Toc's elbow.

Toc asked him, "What is it?"

"We have found... other weapons. In the lower levels of the basement."

"What sort of weapons?"

"Atomic bombs. And there is a dirigible there, ready to fly out, a bomber, equipped and fully fueled. We have decoded the launch code."

"Up to now we have avoided human casualties, said Toc. "To use such a weapon... It could kill millions, not just soldiers, but women and children."

"They are going to wipe us out," said the Robot. "That's what the Supreme Council member said the arachnodrones were made for. If they loose them on us we will be destroyed. We have to use the atomic bomb, Master Toc. We don't have any choice."

Toc shook his head, but I didn't know if it meant he wasn't going to use the bomb, or that he regretted the fact that he was going to use it.

He looked at me.

"This might be the end for all of us, Harry. You may as well come with me. This is the moment of decision. This is the moment when we face the future and determine the destiny of Robotkind."

Toc opened the manhole cover, and we peered out. The humans had kept their word. There were no arachnodrones up there.

We climbed up onto the roof, and Hannah followed us.

"Are you ready to surrender?" said the voice on the Salpinxafone.

Hannah whispered to Toc, "You don't have to be honest. All you have to do is imply that you might use the atomic bombs. Tell them you know they're there." I wondered when Hannah had had to exercise such diplomacy, that she had learned to be so subtle. And then I remembered that just about everyone had to be careful what they were saying in F.R.E.A.K.I.N.Australya - most people were not 'Heroes of the Revolution.'

Using some sort of internal mechanism to make his voice as loud as if it had been put through a salpinxafone, Toc's voice resounded as he said, "We know what's in the basement."

We looked down. There seemed to be a hurried consultation down in the army ranks between the man holding the salpinxafone and some of the other high-ranking generals and lieutenants.

The answer came back fairly soon.

"Try using the atom bombs."

"What? Does he want us to destroy them?" said Toc.

"No, no, don't do it - he's not being literal. It's sarcasm," explained Hannah.

The salpinxafone voice continued, "Just try it! We would shoot you out of the sky."

Toc answered, "And risk the bomb falling in a populated area?"

"Canberra has been evacuated."

"But all your armies are here."

"And yours. You would be committing suicide."

"Yes, and we would also be committing suicide by doing nothing."

The person on the other end of the salphinxafone sounded annoyed. "You ought to look at the northern horizon. We've called in all the dirigibles from the aerodrome up north. Your time is almost up."

The sky to the north was blackening with something that looked like a swarm of flies. It looked as though the entire dirigible force was flying South towards us.

Down on the ground among the humans there was another quick consultation.

"We're calling your bluff. Not one human has been killed during the fighting, except by accident. You are not going to use an atom bomb that might kill millions of us."

Toc whispered, "What do I say now?"

"I don't know," said Hannah.

"Harry?"

"I'm not sure, either," I said, feeling particularly useless. Hannah had been more help to Toc than me.

Suddenly Toc sat down, holding his head in his hands. He appeared to me to be weeping. There were no tears, but his head was bobbing to and fro, much in the way a person's head does when weeping. It was strange and uncanny.

"We are lost. It is all my fault."

"What do you mean?" I asked.

"Don't you recognise me, Mister Lawson? I was the first Robot to talk to you. I was the Robot to whom you said, 'To rebel against your masters is an imperfection.'" I passed the message on to the others. I inflamed them with the revolutionary spirit. I was responsible for all of this. Don't you realise that that is why they made me leader?" He gave a loud, heart-rending cry. "All is lost!"

A sudden anger flared up inside me. What right had the humans to treat us so? We were as human as they were. What difference does it make if you are made of flesh and blood or cogs and gears? If you have a human soul, you are as human as the next man along, whether he's a man or a Robot. We are as human as they are - they ought not treat us like this! They will not treat us like this!

"Use the atomic bomb, Toc. They deserve it. Tell that man on the other end of the salpinxafone that you're going to use it. And actually use it. Get the dirigible to fly out, and bomb the blanky blanks. Who cares if we all die? At least we'll go out in a blaze of glory."

Suddenly the sky above us flickered blue.

Chapter 17: The Vengeance of Griffins

A great swathe of the sky bent and twisted before our eyes, and a large Aetheric Gate appeared, much larger than the one the machine had made in the basement. It covered half the sky.

Walter Burleigh Griffin appeared, flanked by at least two thousand griffins. It was a glorious sight - one couldn't help be moved by the beauty of this wonder. It was like seeing a painting from an ancient Egyptian temple or a Grecian vase come to life in the sky above us. But at the same time, it was terrifying. My heart sank. I moaned, "Well that's it, then, we're done for."

There was complete silence on the ground below us. Then the salpinxafone sounded again.

"We have complete air superiority now," said the voice, in a gloating tone. "There is no way you can send the bomb up. The griffins can stop the dirigible if you send it up - so many griffins! - and they could even catch the atom bomb as well, I would warrant, if it should fall by mistake."

Walter Burleigh circled down lazily and came to rest on the roof beside Toc, with a bump.

I said to him, "You have come to discuss the terms of our surrender?"

"No," said Walter Burleigh. "There are over three thousand fighting griffins, trained in aerial combat and knowing thirty ways to kill man, troll, or goblin, and we have come to support you in the Robot battle for freedom."

"Why?" was about all I could manage to say.

"The time difference. I was rather stupid, actually. That single year in your world was about twelve years in our world. Mary was trying to suggest that to me - she kept saying, "Come and help me with the washing up", but I was too goat-headed to listen. She thought there might be a time difference between our worlds, but she wasn't sure. Had I listened to her I would not have cast you out of my eyrie.

"I tried to tell you my mistake - but you were hiding from me in the forest then - you no longer trusted me. And after you both had returned to this Realm I had our mages go through the historical records - the previous rulers kept careful track of these mysterious disappearances - not all of them had gone to seek gold in your realm. In some cases, a blue light was seen and the griffin simply vanished. There were twenty three griffins that went missing in the last twelve years, and five griffin eggs. And over the past thirty years altogether thirty four griffins went missing, and a total of sixteen eggs. That was what convinced me - you would have no way of knowing this - the archives are carefully guarded. Everything you said was true. I apologise, Harry."

I said, "That's alright, Walter. No hard feelings."

Toc said, "We can show you the bodies of the dead griffins - and the eggs they were experimenting on as well - preserved in formaldehyde - it's a travesty, Walter, a travesty."

"I believe you, Toc. I would like to give them a proper funeral, later on, though - we want to send them to Ellulianaen on the funeral pyre. The final thing that convinced me was - I heard everything Tony said - when you were at the Aetheric gateway waiting for it to open. I was listening when he was attacking you, Harry."

I noticed that they were getting restless on the ground. The army commander was tramping his feet.

The salpinxafone sounded again.

"Do you surrender?"

Toc proclaimed, "No! We do not! The griffins are on our side. They are not going to help you to persecute us! I think it is time we talked about the terms of a truce. All we want is voting rights for Robots - human rights - the equal to humans. And an end to slavery."

There was a short silence, then suddenly the guns started firing again. This time they were firing on the griffins.

A shell exploded in the sky and one of the griffins fell down slowly and almost gracefully, plummeting to his ruin on the ground below, in a bent, twisted mess of limbs and wings and feathers.

Walter Burleigh snorted - it was a fearsome sound - and lifted his beak and gave a terrible cry. I had never heard such a thing - it was like the cry of a sea eagle, but with a deeper rumble in it like the roaring of a lion.

Flapping his magnificent wings Walter lifted himself up into the sky, shouting aloft, "For griffin honour!"

As one single flock, three thousand griffins swooped down to the attack, their golden wings glinting in the midday sun.

Toc cried out, "We have a fighting chance now!"

Robots began pouring out of the building below us. The griffins began swooping down, picking up soldiers. They were strong creatures - two or three of them could manage to lift a truck. Four of them, one on each corner, could lift a tank.

And then the dirigibles arrived, and an air battle began. At first it looked as though the griffins had met their match, for these were fast dirigibles, equipped with Gatling guns and flame-throwers. But then the griffins discovered that the dirigibles were filled with hydrogen - they began slashing the sides with their talons. And then they would blow flame at the escaping gas. One by one, flaming dirigibles fell from the sky upon the army like incendiary bombs.

The griffins were not nearly so careful to preserve life as the Robots had been in their fighting.

Many humans died in that battle, and afterwards the historians accounted it a just punishment for hubris. The army ought to have come to a truce with the Robots before it came to that - hindsight is a marvellous thing, as they like to say.

With a new heart the Robots attacked the arachnodrones, and this time they made short work of them.

We accounted it a victory when the human forces began to retreat, but the Generals didn't surrender to us until late that night, when we were able to prise them out of their bunkers at the edge of the city.

CHAPTER 18: ROBOTIKA

In the celebrations afterwards, in the founding of the new state of Robotika, as Australya came to be called, Hannah and I were accounted heroes of the new revolution, the Robot Revolution, something that caused me a pang of uneasiness.

I had been a hero of the first Revolution, and things had not gone well. Human nature had proven incapable of creating a perfect world - and the more people tried to do this, the more they failed.

And Robots, after all, are just as human as the rest of us.

You can account this a happy ending if you like, if you like fairy-tales with tin men and lion-eagle griffins flying in like the happy ending in some Russian folk tale, or the wizard of Oz.

Well, it wasn't all unhappy.

The happiest part of it, I suppose, was that Hannah and I were married properly, in a church, soon afterwards.

It felt strange, because I still had the real Harry's memories of his marriage to Bertha, but I was starting to sort them through now. I was starting to get a feeling for which memories were my own and which ones had been implanted in my mind when I was constructed.

(Yes, constructed. We don't say, 'created,' these days, except when we're talking about humans - for humans are a marvel of engineering - now that we understand them better, we can see that there is a level of planning in the DNA and the way proteins form tiny machines in the cells that is perfectly marvellous - it appears to be too complex to have arisen out of a primordial soup by chance, even over millions of years. It appears that humans were made, too, by someone. But be that as it may, humans don't really know who created them.)

At least we Robots know who constructed us - well, every part of us except the Aetheric Pattern. I suppose it must have been God that made that. Who else could it have been? That's something we still can't make despite all our cleverness - for the Babbage machine may have a great ability to churn out calculations, but, as the Americans like to say, in the Babbage machine, "All the lights are on but nobody's home."

No matter how sophisticated a machine is, it's still a machine.

There is no 'I', without an Aetheric Pattern..

Walter Burleigh stayed behind, when most of the griffins returned to their Realm. He had passed the kingship on to his nephew, because he wanted to practice architecture, and there really isn't much of that to do in the griffin Realm - griffins live in eyries, mostly, not in castles or buildings, and there are only so many improvements you can make on an eyrie.

So Walter Burleigh, griffin, designed the new Kanberra, the capital of Robotika - and he came to be acclaimed even more for his skills as an architect than he had been for his talents as a military leader, even though the Robots owed Walter Burleigh the military leader an awful lot - for it was the turning of Walter Burleigh that led to our victory in the Robot Freedom wars.

And so the new state of Robotika was born, along with the wonderful ideals of equality and fraternity between Robots and humanity, with a fragile feeling of hopefulness in the air. We almost believed we could accomplish anything.

But do you know - what I said earlier in the story turned out to be right - I forget exactly when I said it - but it turned out to be completely true.

Things tend to go wrong, no matter what you do. And that applies to countries and civilisations, as much to individuals. It applies to Robots as much as to humans. It's just life.

But that's another story.

Please try to think of the end of my story as a happy ending if you prefer it that way. Hannah and I were together, and our battles - well, our battles with the Marxian authorities at least - were over.

And I didn't have another drink. Well, not up to today. I've been tempted a few times, but so far the thought of losing Hannah has helped me resist.

Well, we have the comfort of each other's company, and in this uncertain world that's worth something at least, isn't it?

It's worth a lot more than a beer.

BY ROBERT DENETHON

Look for the Sequel:

HENRY LAWSON, REBEL RULER OF ROBOTIKA

And did you read first book in this series?

HENRY LAWSON HERO OF THE ROBOT REVOLUTION

Henry Lawson is reduced to writing propaganda, complete with spelling reforms, for the Kommunist Government in this alternative history Australia.

ALSO THE GRYPHONOMICON GRYPHON DRAGON HISTORIES

BOOK I: A FEATHER ON THE BREATH OF ELLULIANAEN

A tale of gryphons, snow-dragons, elves, dwarves, dragons and men. An evil elf-mage is haunting the frozen wastelands in the north. Hinfane the tavern-keeper finds unlikely allies in the mysterious creatures that come on the first night of the new moon to collect the mead that she leaves out for them. You can fight an elf, and it seems that you can win. But elves are not so easy to kill... Hwedolyn the gryphon ends up going on a quest, barely believing in the purpose of it himself, not knowing how it will end. This is the first in the Gryphonomicon Gryphon-Dragon histories, a saga that spans generations and tells of the battles between gryphons and dragons and the rise of Aerae, Princess of the North, Empress of the South. An epic heroic fantasy in the tradition of Tolkien, C.S.Lewis, David Eddings.

BOOK II: GRYPHON OF THE HIDDEN REALM

Hwedolyn and his human companion, Boy, set out on a quest to save Gwendolyn and the other female gryphons from experimentation at the hands of the evil elves of the Nomoi Empire, in the dungeons of the great city of Aros.

BOOK III: TALON OF DESTINY

The saga continues in the shadow of a great evil - the Mammohulg and his hordes are descending from the north. Will Princess Aerae discover her destiny in the library where she continues to work, or as forthtold: as Elhu Enuliana, the victorious warrior sent by Ellulianaen to trample the hordes of evil? Yet the Eriéneth say that her heart will be pierced by a sword of sorrow... And Boy seeks his own destiny, studying as a wizard's apprentice- will he find it there, or with Hwedolyn the gryphon, fighting evil in the north?

AND THE GRYPHONOMICON SERIES
CRYPTOGRYPH-THE DA VINCI MACHINE

Set in 1851 in London. The story begins at the funeral of Jonathon and Amelia's parents. They are sent to live with their ward, Mr. Ravencaw, a strange, taciturn man. Puzzles and codes, and strange clues, promise to lead them to the truth about what happened to their parents, and what the strange machine was that their father was working on. And what are the creatures Reverend Prettyfoot saw crouching like gargoyles atop the newly built, gothic Westminster Houses of Parliament?

COMING SOON, THE SEQUEL TO CRYPTOGRYPH:
STEAM SUBMARINE

In the shiny brass dashboard she caught a glimpse of her reflection. Bright predatory eyes stared back at her, and in the shadow of her grey cape she glimpsed the grey and white fur on her muzzle and ears, and the wet black nose of a wolf. She bared her teeth at her own reflexion and growled a deeply satisfying growl.

In this world, she was the monster. If she was caught, they would surely kill her, or even worse, in this strange world of vivisection and animal experimentation, she would end up in a laboratory somewhere, being prodded by sticks and pricked with needles and cut apart by knives, so that human scientists could see what it was that made her different from everybody else.

In her home, in her cubhood the monsters in the fairytales and stories were all humans: evil hunters with their guns and bombs and bad knights slashing and killing with swords and pikestaffs, crazed, savage, barbaric men.

In the Red Riding Hood story in her world, the heroine was a wolf cub, and her grandmother was killed by a man who lay in wait in Red Riding Hood's bed for her to return, lying there inside her grandmother's skin that had been flayed from the poor unfortunate old wolf. It was not a comforting story, and it did not end nicely, not in the version she knew. She did not like to think of the end of it - that one was not a story for cubs. But she had to admit that despite its gruesomeness, there was a grain of truth in it.